Sunny Sweet
Is So NOT Sorry

SUNNY SWEET
Is So NOT Sorry

Jennifer Ann Mann

illustrated by Jana Christy

BLOOMSBURY
NEW YORK   LONDON   NEW DELHI   SYDNEY

First published in the United States of America in October 2013
by Bloomsbury Children's Books
www.bloomsbury.com

For information about permission to reproduce selections from this book, write to
Permissions, Bloomsbury Children's Books, 1385 Broadway, New York, New York 10018
Bloomsbury books may be purchased for business or promotional use.
For information on bulk purchases please contact Macmillan Corporate and
Premium Sales Department at specialmarkets@macmillan.com

Library of Congress Cataloging-in-Publication Data
Mann, Jennifer Ann.
Sunny Sweet is so not sorry / by Jennifer Ann Mann.
pages   cm
Summary: Follows eleven-year-old Masha and her "evil genius" little sister,
Sunny, through one very adventurous day, as Masha faces scary situations, meets
new people, and gains new insight into life with her hardworking, single mother.
ISBN 978-1-59990-977-6 (hardcover) • ISBN 978-1-61963-046-8 (e-book)
[1. Sisters—Fiction. 2. Genius—Fiction. 3. Single-parent families—Fiction. 4. Russian
Americans—Fiction. 5. Adventure and adventurers—Fiction.] I. Title.
PZ7.M31433Su 2013   [Fic]—dc23   2013015362

Book design by John Candell
Typeset by Westchester Book Composition
Printed and bound in the U.S.A. by Thomson-Shore Inc., Dexter, Michigan
2 4 6 8 10 9 7 5 3 1

All papers used by Bloomsbury Publishing, Inc., are natural, recyclable products
made from wood grown in well-managed forests. The manufacturing processes
conform to the environmental regulations of the country of origin.

To Maria Hykin

SUNNY SWEET
Is So NOT Sorry

Waking Up on the Wrong Side of the Bed

I was sound asleep when my head itched. Somehow my sleeping brain sent the message to my fingers to go scratch it. And they went. But they certainly didn't expect to find what they did when they got there. I wasn't sleeping anymore. I sat up. Or at least I tried to, but my head was weirdly heavy. And not because I was still tired, *but because my pillow was stuck to it!*

"Huh?"

You know how you have places for things in your brain? Places like where your favorite breakfast stuff hangs out. Or the place where you keep the memory of building that cool fort out of old wood and cardboard boxes. Or the corner where you just crammed all the information you need for the gigantic test you have in Mrs. Hull's fifth-grade science class. But nowhere in my brain was there a place for this moment . . . waking up on a Thursday morning with my pillow pasted to my right ear.

I ripped the pillow off as if it were a Band-Aid—hard and fast. It's a lie, by the way, that pulling something off fast doesn't hurt. It does. But I mostly forgot about my throbbing head when I saw what was stuck to my purple-flannel pillowcase: a big clump of long hair (my hair!) and a giant purple daisy. My hands grabbed my head where that clump of hair had just been, and now my fingers knew exactly what they were feeling . . . plastic flowers!

I jumped out of bed and ran to the mirror that hung over my dresser. "Holy moly crocatoly!" My head was some sort of Thanksgiving Day table decoration!

I heard the soft pattering of six-year-old feet approach my door. Sunny peeked in. I looked down at her, and she looked back at me, and I knew. I just knew. Maybe it was the roundness of her eyes as she blinked at me. Or maybe it was the way she stood so still, like a deer that had just heard a twig snap. Or maybe it was the sound of her voice when she said, "Good morning, Masha," like she was some proper little English kid.

And she knew I knew . . . because she took a slow step back into the hallway.

I lunged but that tiny little toothpick body of hers was too quick, and she took off down the hall toward our mother's room.

"Get back here!" I screamed. "What did you do?"

* * *

I busted through the bedroom door to find Sunny cowering behind my mother. "Masha, what's going on? I'm trying to get ready for . . ." but then my mom stopped and stared.

"She did it!" I screeched, pointing at my little sister.

"Calm down, Masha," my mother said, but I could see her hiding a smile behind her hand.

Sunny wasn't hiding anything. She broke into ear-piercing giggles as she slid backward into my mother's closet, her tiny body disappearing behind a row of shiny dresses.

"Mom!"

"Okay," my mother said, turning and reaching

4

through a hundred soft sleeves to retrieve my sister. "Sunny, explain yourself."

"Explain yourself?" I cut in. "How can you *explain* this cornucopia of horror stuck to my head?"

"That isn't a cornucopia," Sunny said, pointing at my head. "A cornucopia is a horn-shaped basket filled with fruits and vegetables."

My mother got down on one knee. "Do you know where the first cornucopia came from?" she asked.

"Greek mythology," my sister answered.

"WHY ARE WE HAVING SOME SORT OF LEARNING MOMENT WHEN I HAVE PLASTIC FLOWERS STUCK TO MY HEAD?"

I shouted so loudly that I hurt my own ears, and Sunny scampered out of the room like a squirrel up a tree. Then, all out of steam, I flopped onto my mother's bed. The plastic flowers immediately got tangled up in her crocheted bedspread, so even this act of frustration—flinging myself onto my mother's bed— became frustrating. My little sister is the devil!

I know that lots of kids have annoying little brothers and sisters. I've been around; I've seen them. Take my cousin Suki: she has my little cousin Bruce to deal with. Bruce is always trying to lick people, and my aunt Lila makes us play air hockey with him for hours when I visit. But Bruce also lets Suki have anything she wants out of his Easter basket, and he never tells his mom when Suki pretends to eat her peas but is really just spitting them one by one into her milk.

Sunny would tell.

And Sunny wouldn't stop with just telling on me; she'd take it a step further and *discuss* it with my mom—like why she thinks I did what I did, pretending to be some kind of doctor. And you know why? Because she *is* some kind of doctor! Well, not exactly a doctor, but a genius. She was born brilliant. And normally I would just be like, good for her, you know, go, genius girl, go, but she also happened to be born evil . . . making her an evil genius. And I know that the day is coming when she'll invent some poisonous gas that will snuff out the sun and freeze us all into human Popsicles, but until that time, she seems perfectly content to practice her evil schemes on me.

"Okay, Masha, you're right." My mother sighed as she bent over me and started disconnecting my head from her bedspread. But her tone made me feel like she didn't really believe I *was* right. I hated when she did that—said something that seemed like she was on my side but actually sounded like she felt the opposite. "Wow," she whispered as she worked, "these things are really glued in there."

I moaned.

My cell phone began ringing from down the hall. It was probably Sunny. Sunny always called my cell. When it stopped ringing and then started again, I knew it was my little sister. Only Sunny would do that too! Sunny loves her cell phone, and not because she likes talking to people, but because she loves things like radio frequencies and voice channels and duplex connections and other tools of her evil trade. I didn't get to have my own cell phone until this Christmas, when I turned eleven years old. And two presents after I opened mine, Sunny opened hers—and she's only six years old! My mother said Sunny's phone was just for emergencies. Yeah, right, like Sunny is going to dial 911 when she blows up the earth.

Just as my mother was finishing untangling the last flower from her bedspread, my cell phone rang a third time. "Sunny," my mom yelled down the hall, "cut it out!"

Even my mother knew that it was Sunny calling me. We moved from Pennsylvania to New Jersey last year after my mom divorced my dad. I'd been going to my new school for almost eight months, but the only person who called me, *ever*, was Sunny. And even though this was the truth, it still completely annoyed me that my mom assumed that the only "friend" I'd made since the move was my very own sister.

"I'm going to bury you in the backyard like a dog bone when Mom's not looking!" I said to Sunny as

8

she skipped back into the room with her cell phone pressed to her ear.

My mother pursed her lips and turned to my little sister. "Sunny, what did you do?"

"SHE GLUED A BUNCH OF PLASTIC FLOWERS TO MY HEAD!" I shouted.

I shout a lot. I can't help it. Sunny makes me. She sets things up so that even Martin Luther King Jr. would have broken down and popped someone right in the nose.

"Shush, Masha," my mother said without turning to look at me. Maybe if she did turn and look at me she'd see the big blooming reason I can't "shush"! But she doesn't turn and look. She never does. Her eyes are always too busy focusing on Sonya Sweet.

That is my sister's full name, although we never call her Sonya; we just call her Sunny. My dad started it. It was on the day that Sonya first came home from the hospital, you know, before we knew she was Darth Vader. I don't really remember it because I was just five years old, but I remember the story. And sometimes the retelling of a story over and over again gets it stuck so tightly in your head that it turns into a real event that you actually remember happening.

My dad said it had rained the entire month before Sonya was born, and then rained all through my mother's giving birth to her, and then through the two days that she and my mom were in the hospital. It rained so much that there was all this flooding and everyone was nervous about water in their basements and dams breaking. I do remember that we didn't have school for two days because the roof of the school was leaking. My dad was the principal and he had canceled school so no one would get hurt. I loved it when my dad called off school. It made me a hero on the school bus the next day. All the older kids would give me high-fives and knuckle punches, like I'd saved the world from zombies.

When the morning came that Sonya and my mom were due to come home from the hospital, the sun burst out so hot and strong that my dad said the whole town sighed a giant sigh all together. He said that Sonya had brought the sun. And after that, "Sunny" just stuck.

My name is Masha Sweet, and I don't know what the weather was like on the day that I came home from the hospital. Masha is Russian for "Maria." My mom was born in Russia and came to the United States back when she was my age.

"Sunny?" she asked again. "Tell Mommy why you did this to Masha."

"I wanted to make her pretty," Sunny answered, her face lit up by the fakest glow of love you ever saw.

"Oh." My mom sighed, like it was so cute—as if what mini-Vader did was to help me!

"SHE'S NOT EVEN SORRY!" I screamed, and I couldn't stop myself from leaping at Sunny's throat.

My mom's stockings ripped as she held me back from strangling my little sister.

Jumping In

I sat shivering in the green chair in the corner of the living room. My hair was sopping wet and soaking through my favorite panda pajamas, and plastic flowers were still solidly stuck to my head. The green chair is where my mother used to give me time-outs when I was, like, two years old. And yes, I admit that I had been getting a little loud. So would you if you had just spent fifteen minutes with your nose pressed to the drain at the bottom of the kitchen sink while your mother practically scrubbed your scalp off. But still, I am *way* too old for a time-out.

Anyway, my mom thought it would be a good idea if I sat and "calmed down." I told her that I would totally "calm down" as soon as this flower arrangement was off my head! But now I've decided to sit quietly because I could see my mom was getting upset. And I hate it when she gets upset.

Sunny came slithering down the hallway.

"Go away," I growled.

She didn't listen. She never does. It's what makes Sunny so evil. She tortures me and then hangs around, not seeming to get the fact that she tortured me.

She came right up to my chair and leaned over, reaching out to my head.

"Don't touch me," I told her, pulling my flowers away. I stared straight ahead of me, making a point of not looking at her.

"Remember that Halloween," she said, "when Daddy took that box and pasted a tablecloth over it and then pasted plastic plates to it? And plastic cups and plastic forks and plastic knives and plastic spoons and napkins, but not plastic napkins, those were paper. And he made bacon and pancakes, and we glued them to the plates. And he got an old hat of his and then we glued lots of flowers to the hat. And then he cut a hole in the top of the box, right in the middle, and I stuck my head through and wore the hat with the flowers glued to it."

I remembered, but I was not speaking to her.

"I was a breakfast table!" she yelled. "Remember? Everybody loved it, especially the dogs. Remember the dogs jumping at me because they really wanted that bacon? I got knocked over by a hundred dogs that night. What were you for Halloween that year? Oh, I remember," she said. "You were a mime."

"I was a bank robber," I said.

"Are you sure?" she asked, staring at me with her giant blue eyes. "I think you were a mime. Remember, you were all dressed in black and had that black hat on." The fact that Sunny really seemed to remember me as a mime just made me want to strangle her even more.

"Mom! I'm going to be late for school and miss my test in science!" I shouted into the kitchen, making Sunny jump.

14

My test wasn't until after lunch, but still, I didn't want to show up to school late. Just the thought of showing up late made me feel sweaty. And I knew that I wouldn't get over that sweaty, late feeling by lunchtime. I liked things to happen the way they were

supposed to happen. You know, like showing up for school at the time you were supposed to show up for school. Sitting in time-out with a sopping-wet garden glued to the top of my head with Sunny chatting away about Halloween was a pretty solid example of how things were *not* supposed to happen.

"I'm trying to think," my mother called from the kitchen.

"She's thinking," Sunny repeated, like I was deaf as well as stupid.

"CALL THE DOCTOR!" I shouted.

"Masha," my mother yelled back, "Stop shouting!"

"But anyway, I made the glue myself," Sunny said, sitting on the arm of my chair. "Move over."

I purposely spread out farther, taking up as much pillow space as I could. There is an entire other chair in the room—and a couch. Sunny always wants to sit half on top of me.

"I bet those two girls at school that you always talk about—what are their names?—anyway, I bet they'll love your flowers," Sunny said, reaching out again to try and touch a bloom.

I snapped my head away from her finger and glared at her. Sunny was talking about Nicole Sims and Alex Ruez. Nicole and Alex were model fifth graders. They didn't have a single clothing mistake in their entire closets. They got sky-high grades in all their classes. They played sports without doing some silly sliding split when they went to catch a ball. They even did extra things like playing the cello and singing solos in the chorus. Everyone knew Nicole and Alex. And just the thought of the two of them standing in the hallway of Seward Elementary watching me pass by with my head full of plastic flowers made all the air in my lungs vanish . . . leaving me just enough to yell directly into Sunny's evil little face, "Go away!"

She fell backward off the arm of the chair and then jumped up and turned herself around in one motion, taking off down the hallway out of my sight.

My mother walked into the room with her cell phone pressed to her ear and a "you'd better calm down" look boring into my soul. She spoke politely into the phone, "Yes, good morning. This is Jane Sweet. How are you? Yes, of course I'll hold." That's when I remembered that I had decided to sit quietly so I wouldn't upset her.

I pulled my backpack up on my lap so I could open my *Longman Active Study English-Chinese Dictionary* without taking the book out of my bag. I was learning Mandarin Chinese but didn't want my mom or Sunny to know. Back at my old school, they had just begun to offer Chinese. It had been my dad's idea. Since I was a good Spanish student, I had been chosen to begin the new language classes. But then we moved. They didn't offer Chinese in my new school, so I decided to "borrow" the book and learn it by myself. I kept it a secret because Sunny would have just learned Chinese in a week and spoiled the whole language for me. The only one who knew my secret was my neighbor, Mrs. Song. She was really patient, even when it took me a ton of times to say something right.

Sunny crawled back into the room on her hands and knees, and I shoved my Chinese dictionary into my backpack. She made her way over to my mother. "Who are you calling, Mom?" she asked.

My mother held her finger to her lips to quiet her. "Yes, hello. Well, I'm not sure," she said into the phone. "Maybe I should speak with the nurse?"

"She's calling the doctor," Sunny said to me, like I didn't get it. I zipped up my backpack and let it slide to the floor, ignoring her.

"Masha?" she said.

When I didn't look at her, Sunny repeated herself over and over again, with just a tiny pause between each time, "Masha . . . Masha . . . Masha," until I finally stared over at her.

"Mom's calling the doctor," she said.

"Shhh," I hissed with my eyebrows locked together.

"Hi, Barbara, how are you? It's Jane Sweet."

Silence . . . followed by my mom's fake laughter. I'm sure Nurse Barbara just made some "sour" joke. People are always making sweet-and-sour jokes when we say our name. They can't help themselves. Last summer, when we first moved here, I had to hear so many sweet-and-sour jokes that I stopped even giving people that little smile you're supposed to give some-one telling a bad joke. I'd heard them all . . . fifty times. People back in Pennsylvania were used to our name because it was my dad's name and he'd grown up in that town, just like me. Plus, he was in charge of the whole school, Principal Sweet, and everyone loved him, so "Sweet" just fit him naturally and wasn't funny.

"Well, Barbara, we're having a rough morning. It's Masha . . ."

I opened my mouth in horror. It's not me, it's her . . . the scrawny little being that plots world destruction standing right next to you!

"There was a bit of an accident with some glue and plastic flowers."

Silence.

"Yes, plastic flowers. They sort of . . . got stuck in Masha's hair."

I gawked at my mother and flung my body across the green chair. Sort of? Yeah, right, an accident.

I reached up and yanked at "the accident." The

wet mass of plastic was totally and completely glued into my hair. And I have some serious hair. It's dark brown and goes all the way down my back almost to my butt. The flowers were glued into my hair at the very top of my head, close to my roots, so they looked like they grew out of my skull overnight.

My mother sat down on the edge of the couch, fiddling with the hole in her stocking and waiting—I guess—for someone to find "ungluing plastic flowers from heads" in a medical book. Sunny got up from her place on the floor and sat down directly next to my mother, putting her head on my mother's shoulder. My mom lifted her arm and put it around Sunny. The urge came over me to use the throw pillow from my chair just as its name suggests.

"Yes, I'm here," my mom said into the phone. Kissing the top of Sunny's blond head, she stood up and wandered over to the front window. "Yes. Uh-huh. A goldfish? That sounds awful. Uh-huh. Yes, I've heard of the dime up the nose."

WHAT ARE THEY TALKING ABOUT? I

shouted—but only in my head so my mother wouldn't have any trouble hearing when they gave her the secret recipe for getting this stuff off me.

"Okay, yes," she said to the nurse into her cell phone, but her eyes were focused right at me in my green chair. "Thanks so much." She hung up and didn't say anything, but she didn't have to. There was obviously no secret recipe.

"Let's try the freezer," my mother said.

"What?" I whined. But I was up and out of the chair and heading to the kitchen.

"What's in the freezer?" Sunny asked, stumbling at my heels.

My mother thought that freezing the glue might make it possible to crack the flowers off my head. It didn't sound like it was going to work, but I stuck my head in the freezer while my mother changed her stockings and got the pocket-sized Dr. Frankenstein ready for school. The freezer reminded me of Antarctica, and not just because of the lonely coldness of it, but because it was such an alien place. I really hadn't spent much time in the freezer before. I laid my head

22

on a box of frozen pizza, and after ten minutes of staring at dirty ice cube trays my mother checked back in.
First she pulled on a blue one. Then she yanked at a
pink one. The daisies did not crack off my head.

"What about peanut butter?" my mom suggested.
"That's what they use to get chewing gum out of
hair." I just blinked at her. She turned and reached
for the jar of super-crunchy Skippy.

Sunny Sweet is going to be so sorry!

Crash

Sunny had to go to school, and my mom had to go to work. She had some huge meeting that she was stressed about. She always had some huge meeting she was stressed about. You could never say this to her, though. If you did, she'd remind you about how she's got a lot on her plate, blah, blah, blah, and make you feel all guilty—like it was my big idea to divorce my dad and move to another state.

Luckily Mom agreed that I should stay home. She wiped the last of the peanut butter off my forehead with a wet paper towel and told me to call Mrs. Song next door if I needed anything. Then she promised we'd figure it all out when she got home. Sunny actually begged to stay with me. We go to the same school. And even though it was only three blocks away, my mom always dropped us off in the morning and Sunny and I would meet up after school and walk home together. Sunny hated school. She was in a regular first-grade class with kids her age, but the school pulled her out for a lot of the day and let her work one-on-one with these gifted teachers. Although she still had to be in with the other kids for lunch and recess and stuff. My mother said that it was hard for Sunny to relate to the other kids because she was so advanced and all.

Yeah, right. Maybe it's hard for the other kids to relate to pure evil.

I knew my mom would never let my sister stay home from school. But just in case, I made sure she understood that anyone in the house without plastic flowers glued to her head would be spending the day locked in a closet.

I stayed by the front door even after I couldn't see

my mom's car anymore. I couldn't believe that I was going to miss my science test, but there was no way that I was showing up at my new school like this. I'd been going there for all of fifth grade, but I always thought about it as my "new" school. I wasn't really great friends with anybody there. The girls had known each other since kindergarten and already had their best friends, and even their second-best friends. The boys were, you know, just boys. They went around whipping scrap paper at each other and laughing at absolutely anything that sounded like a fart. I went to school every day, but mostly I don't think anybody noticed me except to ask me stuff about homework. And they only did that if Junchao Tao was absent. Junchao was the second-smartest kid in our school, since of course, Sunny Sweet was the smartest. And of course, Junchao sat right behind me because her last name was "Tao" and mine was "Sweet." It seemed like I always got stuck next to the geniuses. But at least Junchao was a super-quiet brilliant kid, unlike my little sister, who never shut up.

I turned and stared into the front hall mirror.

Well, I bet they would have noticed me today. You don't exactly blend in when you have a bouquet pasted to the top of your head. Reaching up, I plucked a petal from one of the flowers. "I ace the makeup science test." I plucked another. "I ace the makeup science test not." And then another. "I ace the makeup science test . . ."

Crash!

I heard the sound of rattling empty cans and old plastic bottles hopping along the road. It sounded like my neighbor, Mrs. Song, had just backed her car into our garbage cans again. The garbagemen always left the cans sitting right behind her car, and she never remembered to check for them. I opened the front door with a smile on my face because the last petal I had pulled before the crash said I would ace my science test.

When I looked down the front walk I didn't see her car, just our garbage cans all knocked over down by the curb, which was weird. Then a spinning bike tire sticking out from behind the cans caught my eye. I ran down the front steps and out to the sidewalk.

There was Mrs. Song lying in the garbage! Her eyes were closed and she wasn't moving.

I dropped to my knees. "Oh my gosh, Mrs. Song. Mrs. Song, it's me, Masha. Are you okay?"

I bent down into her face. She was breathing. I put my hand on her chest and waited for her heartbeat. I felt a steady knock against my palm. "Your heart's beating, Mrs. Song," I told her. Then I jumped up and looked around for help. The street was empty.

"Help!" I croaked in a loudish whisper. All of a sudden I forgot how to shout. "Help!" I tried again, but the yell got stuck deep in my throat.

I dropped back to my knees. "Mrs. Song, please wake up, wake up. *Qing, qing,*" I tried begging her in Chinese. It meant "please, please." But Mrs. Song wasn't listening. I shook her shoulder a tiny bit, but she still didn't move. "I'll call 911," I told her. "I'll be right back." I watched her for one more second, hoping she'd open her eyes. She didn't.

I ran into the house and up the stairs, and ripped my cell phone from the charger. Then I practically jumped down the entire staircase and just about smashed right through the screen door. Three hops brought me back to the garbage pile. I slid to my knees through some broken eggshells and other gross, wet garbage, and stared down at Mrs. Song. She hadn't woken up—or even moved—in the four seconds that it had taken me to get my cell phone.

All of a sudden the buttons on my phone seemed like tiny dots and my thumb was as thick and wobbly as an uncooked hot dog. Before I could direct my finger to the number 9, the phone rang. I immediately dropped it like it burned me, and it clunked right onto poor Mrs. Song's forehead. Not that she noticed, but still. I scooped up the phone and stared at the screen. The ten numbers were as familiar to me as the freckles on my nose—*Sunny*! I never put Sunny in as a contact because I never, ever wanted to contact her, so her telephone number just came up as numbers. And when you see the same ten digits in a row over and over and over again, they become something together, and this something was a loud groan.

"Sunny, I can't talk right now," I growled into the phone.

"Hi, Masha. Mommy just dropped me at school. I'm walking past the teachers' lounge, you know, the one by the nurse's office."

"Sunny . . ."

"I just saw Mrs. Harris in the front office."

"Sunny, listen to me."

"I just know she's here to substitute for Mr. Fenton today. And that means I'm going to have to spend the whole day with her."

30

"Sunny, I am in an emergency situation."

"I don't think it's an emergency, Masha," she said. "Unless the glue is burning you?"

"The glue can burn?"

"Mrs. Harris is the one who thinks that pi equals a-p-p-l-e," she spelled. "How can I spend a whole day with her?"

I had no idea what Sunny was talking about. I never do.

"Sunny, I'm hanging up!"

"But wait! I'm right on the edge of a hexagonal cell. Stay on the phone with me until I get to the second floor so I can watch the control channel change on the grid."

"Sunny, Mrs. Song had a bike accident and I need to call the ambulance." I hung up on her and immediately dialed 9-1-1.

Calling 911 is so weird. It's just like on TV. The operator is completely calm, even when your neighbor is lying in front of you all sprawled out in kitchen garbage and maybe dying. He took my name and address and then listened to my story about how I found Mrs.

Song and that she was breathing and her heart was beating and stuff. Then he gave me instructions on things I should and shouldn't do. He was in the middle of explaining how to perform CPR if it became necessary, which was freaking me out, when Mrs. Song's eyes fluttered open.

"I gotta go," I told the operator and hung up. "Mrs. Song, what happened? Why were you on a bike? Did you fall? I was so scared."

Mrs. Song blinked a bunch of times and tried to sit up.

"Don't move, Mrs. Song," I told her. At least I remembered one thing the 911 operator told me.

"Masha," she said in her thick Mandarin accent, looking at the coffee grinds on her jacket and the bike seat two inches from her nose. She looked back at me and then reached for my face . . . but then she saw them. "Masha?" she asked, reaching for the flowers as if she thought that once her hand got close, they might disappear.

"Sunny," I explained.

She nodded and dropped her hand to her side.

She understood. Just last week, after Mrs. Song complained that we weren't getting enough rain for her lilacs, Sunny tried to produce rain clouds. And she almost blew up Mrs. Song's house. Of course my mom blamed the whole thing on the chemical company, who took her credit card number over the phone from Sunny and dropped off a truckload of liquid nitrogen in our driveway. My mom never blames stuff on Sunny. Sonya Sweet can never do anything wrong, even when she's mixing up hazardous materials in her sand bucket!

I shoved the garbage away from Mrs. Song's head and then held her hand.

"Ni ma ma work now?" she said, asking if my mom had left for work yet.

"Yeah, she's gone," I told her.

It seemed like forever before we heard the *wop, wop, wop* of the ambulance from down the street. It pulled up in front of us, and two guys jumped out.

"What happened?" asked the first one. The second one went directly to the back doors of the ambulance and pulled out a bag.

I was confused by the question. It looked obvious to me what had happened. "Uh, I think she fell off the bike into the garbage cans," I told them.

Mrs. Song shook her head and reached for me. "Masha, no hit garbage cans," she said.

Mrs. Song's English isn't that good, although she understands everything. Because of this, she always looks like she's a little angry at you, but once you get to know her you realize it's just because she can't get people to understand her. And after a little bit of practice, you really begin to get her. I've lived next to Mrs. Song for almost a year now, so I totally get her.

"What did she say?" asked the first guy, glancing up at my head and then back into my eyes without even a tiny reaction. I guess he sees a lot worse than a kid with plastic flowers stuck to her head. I kind of liked that. He was the "talker." The second guy was the "worker," and he was busy pulling stuff out of the bag and taking Mrs. Song's pulse.

"She said she didn't crash into the garbage cans." I shrugged. That's what she said, but it didn't make sense.

34

Mrs. Song clung to my arm. "Yes, Masha, yes. Get tired, you know. Then here," she said, looking around her.

The talker guy looked at me for the meaning. "She said that she felt tired and then she wound up in the garbage."

"Syncopal episode," said an extremely familiar voice.

"Sunny," I moaned, turning to see my little sister standing on the curb.

"The kid's right," said the worker guy. "Syncopal episode."

Mrs. Song looked at me for what it meant. Of course I didn't know.

"You fainted," Sunny said.

"How did you get out of school?" I snapped.

"I walked," she said.

"That's not what I meant."

"Okay, you two," said the talker guy. "This is still

an emergency situation, and that means we need to get going right now."

They began moving Mrs. Song onto the stretcher.

I picked up Mrs. Song's pocketbook and straw hat out of the garbage and placed them on the stretcher next to her arm. Sunny and I stood side by side as they loaded her up into the ambulance. Before they shut the door, Mrs. Song pulled herself up on the stretcher. "No," she called. "Don't leave children."

Sunny and I turned and looked at each other.

If there had been time to think, maybe I would have thought about the fact that I still had on my panda pajamas and there were a bunch of plastic flowers on my head. And that maybe I didn't want to be jumping into the back of an ambulance for a trip to the hospital with my little sister.

"Let's go, let's go," said the talker guy, rolling his eyes.

But there wasn't time to think.

I grabbed Sunny's hand and jumped in.

Masha, Not Marsha

We told the talker guy our names. His name was Dan, and we gave him all the information we had on Mrs. Song. Sunny even told him that she cooked the best dumplings that anybody ever made. Mrs. Song held on to my hand the entire time, as if at any moment I might disappear from inside the cramped ambulance. It was hard to concentrate on the questions because there was so much to look at. There were a million cabinets jammed full of medical stuff, and radios, and strange equipment with so many straps that I couldn't figure out what part of the body any of these things could be strapped to.

Sunny sat next to Dan and watched as he stuck a needle in Mrs. Song's arm. I couldn't watch. Instead, I looked around the little cab. It was like a cozy, little, moving home. I started thinking about which cabinet I'd put my socks and underwear in if I lived in here, and I wondered if my sweaters would fit on the shelves in the tiny hallway that led to the driver. But then Dan picked up the radio.

"This is 501 reporting . . ."

His voice broke into the comfort of the cab, making my scalp twitch and reminding me of the flowers. "Dan, we gotta go home."

"No!" Sunny said, pumping up the blood pressure cuff to take her own blood pressure for, like, the third time since we got in the ambulance.

"Shush," I told her. "Dan . . ."

He held up his hand. "One minute, Marsha," he said.

"Masha, not Marsha," I said, but he was busy giving his report over the radio.

"What is that peanut butter smell?" called the worker guy from the front of the cab as he pulled us to a stop. I still didn't know his name.

Ugh.

"Dan, we really gotta go home," I repeated.

Neither Sunny nor Dan was listening to me. Sunny had her ears plugged up with Dan's stethoscope, and Dan was busy packaging up Mrs. Song as if he were going to be sending her through UPS. He tucked in her blanket. He wound up the tubes he had inserted into her arm. He tightened the straps across her chest and legs.

The back doors flung open. We were at the emergency room. A breeze blew into the truck, rustling the plastic petals in my hair. I was about to enter the outside world looking like spring had just exploded on top of my head. A moan slipped out from between my lips and I glared at my little sister.

She grinned back at me. "This is great!" she said, like we were about to be dropped off outside the gates of Disney World and not a hospital.

My stomach cramped up, and my head felt wobbly.

Mrs. Song squeezed my hand. She didn't look so good either, and she didn't even have anything stuck to her head!

That's when I remembered Mrs. Song's hat. I quickly picked it up and put it on. It was the wide-brimmed straw hat that she always wore. I pulled the thick red ribbons down under my chin and tied them tight. I could feel the flowers poking into the hat, just as they were poking into my scalp, but at least you couldn't see them. Plus, maybe this would help cut down on the Skippy smell.

I held Mrs. Song's hand all the way into the ER—even while they moved her from the stretcher to the bed. Dan let Sunny carry a plastic bag filled with water attached to the tubing in Mrs. Song's other arm. She held it out in front of her like it was a king's crown on a pillow.

There were a ton of people in the emergency room. Half of them were in blue scrubs, with most of the other half looking like they needed an extra-long bubble bath. This one guy in the bed next to Mrs. Song had a full cast on his leg, from above his knee down to his foot. I've always wanted a cast. At school, if you have a cast you get an elevator key and everyone wants to carry your books. I was right in the middle of having this great daydream of hobbling into Seward Elementary with a cast on my leg and crutches under my arms when Dan said, "See ya, Sunny, Marsha," and swooshed the curtains shut.

"Masha," I whispered.

The happy warmth of the daydream vanished, and I looked down at Mrs. Song. She blinked back at me. She blinked a lot, Mrs. Song, but you got used to it.

"You okay?" she asked. She never spoke Chinese with me in front of Sunny. Somehow she understood it was my secret. Mrs. Song just got stuff like that.

"Yeah, are you okay?"

She squeezed my hand. "Hat looks good on you," she said.

"I like the flowers better," said Sunny, climbing on the chair next to the bed and switching on the little TV-like thing hooked to the wall.

"Don't touch that," I told her. "Get down."

"It's a heart monitor," she said. "I'm going to check Mrs. Song's oxygen level."

"Your oxygen level is going to be zero after I strangle you if you don't turn it off and get down from the chair."

The curtain swooshed open.

"Hello," said a nurse with a doctor behind him.

"What do we have here?" he asked, looking at Sunny.

"I was just about to check her oxygen level," Sunny said.

"How about we take over from here, okay, sweetie?" he said, smiling at Sunny like she was the cutest little thing ever. If only they could all see her crispy little black heart like I could, no one would be smiling.

"I've been studying a lot about anatomy and physiology," Sunny said. "So I can help."

The nurse and doctor chuckled. People were always chuckling at Sunny.

"I'm sure you have," said the doctor as he picked up Mrs. Song's chart, even though I could tell that he was sure she hadn't. Neither of them even looked twice at my giant hat or my panda pajamas.

"Are you three related?" the nurse asked.

"Uh, no, she's our neighbor," I said, moving a little closer to Mrs. Song. "My sister, Sunny, and I came in the ambulance with her."

"Name?" he asked.

"Mrs. Song," I said.

The nurse looked up at me. His eyes looked tired. "*Your* name," he said.

"Oh, uh, Masha," I told him.

"Well, Marsha," he said.

"Masha," I corrected.

"All right, honey," he said, reaching for Sunny's hand. "Why don't you and your sister sit out in the waiting room while we take a good look at your neighbor? And then we'll call you back in, okay?"

"No," whined Sunny, "I want to stay here and help."

"Let us get a quick look," said the doctor. "And then we'll call you right back in. It's only fair since you got a head start on her diagnosis in the ambulance. We need time to catch up."

"Okay," Sunny said. "But don't do any of the good stuff, like the EKG, without me." Sunny turned to me. "An EKG is a test that shows the electrical signals in the heart."

"I know what an EKG is," I said, even though I didn't.

I looked down at Mrs. Song and squeezed her hand. She patted my arm and blinked, letting me know that it was okay, she understood. It's funny how she had held on to my hand for the last half hour, and now I wanted to turn around and hold on to hers. But even though the nurse had made his plan for us to wait outside sound like a question, I knew it wasn't a question. I bent down low and whispered a quick "*zai jian*" in Mrs. Song's ear and let the nurse lead us out to the waiting room.

"Now I want you two to sit right here and don't

move," he said, pointing down at two chairs. We sat.
"You understand, right, Marsha?"

"Yes," I said, not bothering to correct him.

We watched him walk over to a security guard by
the automatic sliding doors that we'd come through
with the stretcher. He pointed at Sunny and me and

said something to the guard. Then the nurse looked back over at us, motioned at the chairs we were sitting in, and said, "Don't move," again from across the room.

I nodded my head.

"Nodding your head is moving," Sunny said.

I jabbed her with my elbow.

"That's moving too," she said.

I turned and glared down at her.

"That too," she squeaked up at me.

I growled.

"Technically, your vocal chords . . ."

"Sunny!" I yelled.

"Okay, Marsha," she said.

Just Sit There

An ER waiting room is such a weird place. All the people are quiet, as if they're in a library, but they aren't working or reading, they're just slumped in chairs. It's like some kind of misery library. There were a bunch of TVs squished into each of the corners of the room, up by the ceiling like big black spiders. All four of the TVs were playing different shows. The loud chatter made my head hurt.

"Maybe we should call Mom," I whispered.

"No," Sunny said. "She'll take me back to school."

"Yes, because that's where you should be. They're probably looking all over for you right now."

"No they're not. I never even went into the classroom. I just walked down past the gym and out the back door. No one even saw me."

"Sunny, you could get in big trouble."

Her giggles made my head feel like it would pop right off my body. Even Sunny knew that she never got in trouble. It didn't matter what she did. Last Christmas Sunny got a rocket set, and the first thing she did was send Eddie, my gerbil, into space. (And by the way, he didn't make it . . . to space or otherwise.) And did she get in trouble? No! She committed gerbil murder and all she had to say was that she had designed a special helmet for him so she thought he would be safe and everyone was like "Oh, Sunny, how thoughtful," and "We'll get you another rocket." No one even cared about poor Eddie. My mom just said, "I'm sure he didn't feel a thing." How does she know what a gerbil feels?

"Anyway, you don't want to bother Mommy at work," Sunny said. She knew that would get me. I didn't want to bother my mother at work. Sunny and I both knew how important Mom's job was to her. Plus, whenever she missed a day of work she always looked way more tired than if she had actually gone and worked all day.

"Well then, just sit there and be quiet," I snapped at her.

She quickly sat back in her chair and stopped talking.

I picked the TV with the Disney Channel playing and started watching.

After about four minutes, Sunny popped up from her seat.

"Don't," I whispered.

"I'm just going to . . ."

"No, you're not just going to do anything," I said. "Let me tell you what is going to happen. We are going to stay right in these chairs until the nurse comes back for us. And then we are going to get Mrs. Song, and Dan and that other guy are going to drive us home.

Okay? So just sit there until the nurse comes back for us."

She frowned and slid back into her chair.

The humming of four different television shows lulled me half asleep. Even in this sleepy state, I saw the boy walk in. He wore a hospital gown and was barefoot, and he stood in the room like he knew he wasn't supposed to be there. He looked like a teenager, but I could tell right away that his mind wasn't that old. Peeking behind himself a couple of times, he looked like a little kid that was just about to steal cookies from the cupboard when he'd been told not to a hundred times. I looked over at security to see if he noticed him too. But the guard's stool was empty.

The boy saw us and gave a little wave. Sunny waved back.

"Don't wave," I said.

"Why not?" she asked.

"Because. We're supposed to be just sitting here."

Sunny twisted away from me in her chair and started to recite the alphabet backward. She always repeated the alphabet backward when she got bored. It was annoying.

After a minute or two, the boy in the hospital gown seemed to forget about not being allowed to be there. He checked out each of the TVs and then unstacked the magazines, but he lost interest in both things pretty quickly. He swung around and scanned the room for something else to do, and his eyes stopped on me.

"I love red!"

My heart jumped and my face got hot as he made his way across the room to us.

"Is red your favorite color?" he asked, pointing at the ribbons of Mrs. Song's straw hat. He stood so close that his knees were almost touching mine. His hospital gown had tiny cowboys riding all over them.

"Her favorite color is orange," Sunny said.

"No, it's not," I said.

"Yes, it is," Sunny insisted. "You wrote in that book you keep under your bed that your favorite color is orange because Daddy's favorite color is orange."

"You read my journal?"

"I wanted to read every book in the house, and that was a book in the house." She shrugged.

I hated when she did that—answered a question that I didn't mean for her to answer.

"I also read your Chinese dictionary for the same reason. Mandarin is really hard to learn, by the way. Every word is a different symbol."

"What? Stay out of my things!"

"But reading your journal gave me the idea to put the flowers in your hair," she said. "You wrote a bunch of times that the girls in school don't ever pay attention to you. I was going to make them look at you."

"You smell like a peanut butter sandwich," said the boy. "I love peanut butter sandwiches."

"She loves this boy named Anton in a book she's reading," Sunny said, giggling. "That was in the journal too."

"You little germ," I said, jumping out of my chair. "That stuff is private!"

"My name's Calvin," said the boy. "What's your name?"

52

"Her name is Marsha," said Sunny, sliding to the floor laughing.

I leaped at her. She scooted around behind the boy. I chased her. Every time I got to the front of the boy, Sunny got around to the back, and every time I got around back, she darted in front of him. I stopped short and turned back the other way and grabbed her. I could hear the boy honking with laughter.

"Calvin, save me," Sunny cried.

"Okay," said the boy.

"Calvin," cried a nurse from behind us, "don't . . ."

Calvin grabbed Sunny and me together in a big bear hug, and we fell to the waiting room floor.

The nurse came running over. She had on rubber gloves and a mask over her face, as if she had just run out of surgery. And she wasn't alone; there was a group of nurses behind her all dressed the same with masks and gloves. They surrounded Calvin, and, speaking gently to him, led him away. Then one of the masked nurses reached for Sunny and me.

"You'll have to come with us too, girls," she said, taking my arm.

"But Mrs. Song . . ." I tried to jerk away from her.

"You can sing us a song on the way up in the elevator," she said.

There were a bunch of them now, and they were surrounding us.

"Sunny!"

I reached for my little sister, but she was already gone.

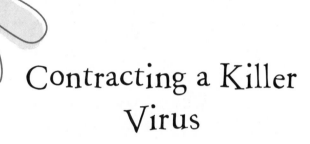

Contracting a Killer Virus

I was bustled down a bunch of halls and into an elevator. I had no idea what was going on or where Sunny or the boy in the hospital gown had gone. The soft, happy music playing in the elevator made me feel sure that something horrible was about to happen to me. I could hear the beeping of the passing floors but couldn't see anything because I was surrounded by people in blue. They seemed to take turns telling me that everything was going to be fine.

When the doors opened, they shuffled me down a

hall, into a room, and up onto a bed. I curled up in a ball and waited for the sound of a chain saw or the glint of a giant knife. Instead, one of the blue people turned and handed me an apple juice and a package of saltines. I love saltines.

Another blue person explained that it wasn't exactly a killer virus, but it was a virus with a funny name, whooping cough. And Calvin had it. They said that Sunny and I probably had shots for it when we were little—which meant we couldn't catch it. But because Sunny and I had rolled around on the floor with Calvin, they had to check just to be sure. They said that Sunny was next door and that they were taking great care of her. They told me that they would put us back together as soon as they got done with a few tests. I nodded like I cared, but really I was fine with getting a break from Sunny. I couldn't believe she had read my journal and found my Chinese dictionary! That was my stuff. I didn't go messing with her stupid ScienceWiz Physics kit, or touch her precious ultraviolet science goggles.

They made me change out of my pajamas and into

a pink hospital shirt and pants that had tiny elephants all over them, but at least I wasn't in a hospital gown like poor Calvin. Then they said they'd call my mother. I gave them our home phone and said that I would try to remember my mom's work number. I actually really didn't know it by heart because I always just hit number 2 on my cell phone, and my cell phone was back in the garbage where I left it by accident. But the truth was that I wasn't trying to remember it. If we ended up having some sort of virus, okay, then we'd call her. Anyway, I knew that Sunny remembered Mom's work number because Sunny remembered everything. I also knew that she would pretend that she didn't because she wouldn't want to go back to school.

At first, being quarantined was pretty cool. I put the Disney Channel back on and sat in bed eating crackers and drinking apple juice. But then the team of masked people showed back up, and the equipment they carried in with them made me kind of nervous. It looked like blood-taking stuff.

"Hi, sweetie," said one of the nurses. "Everything is going to be fine. We're just here to collect a quick

sample so we can make sure you're safe from whooping cough."

Another nurse asked, "What's your name, honey?"

Their voices sounded funny coming from behind the masks.

"Masha," I said.

"Well, Marsha, why don't you take off your hat?" said one nurse.

I shook my head no.

"We're going to have to take that off," came the masked reply.

One of them untied the hat and whisked it off. The hospital air on my head made me shiver.

"Okay," said one of the muffled people, "should we ask?"

"My little sister did it," I mumbled.

"Yikes," said yet another muffled person tugging at one of the blooms, "these things are really glued in there." Even though I couldn't see their mouths, I could feel every single one of them smiling behind their masks.

I sighed through clenched teeth.

I guess some of the other muffled people didn't believe the first muffled person. It was like everyone had to take a turn trying to yank a flower or two out of my hair to prove that they were really stuck in there. They were.

"Maybe we should have the hospital barber take a look at this," one of them suggested.

"Is there such a thing as a hospital barber?" I asked.

But I stopped thinking about the barber because they started explaining things I didn't want to hear, like taking blood for tests, and they began to wrap that rubber band around my arm and search for my vein. I really liked my blood right where it was—inside me. The needle hovered over my arm, and I could feel all my blood vessels screaming, "Not me, not me, not me!"

Ouch.

Contracting a Killer Virus . . . Not

They figured out within an hour that Sunny and I had gotten the shots against "Calvin's disease." This is what I decided to call the virus as I ate my third packet of crackers. Whooping cough just sounded way too silly when I practiced saying it, as if I were telling Mrs. Hull why I had missed her big test.

I asked where Sunny was, and one of the now unmuffled nurses said that she was fine and that she'd gone on rounds with Calvin's orthopedist, the doctor that helps with people's bones.

"Whooping cough hurts your bones?"

"No," said the nurse, smiling. "Calvin also has cerebral palsy, a disorder that can affect how you move. Your sister said she was interested in this condition."

Of course she did.

The nurse told me to finish up my orange juice. (I got bored with apple. You always get bored with apple.) Then she said she'd send in the barber to take a look at the wreath of daisies on my head. She mentioned that they were still trying to get in touch with my mom. I had given them a couple of fake telephone numbers, and they'd taken off happy. I was pretty happy too. I mean, how often do you meet a medical barber? He was exactly what I needed.

I was sucking down the rest of my juice and thinking about how lucky I was that Calvin's favorite color was red when my medical barber walked in. His initial reaction went something like, "Whoa! Lord have mercy," and things didn't seem as promising as they had two minutes before. The next five minutes of head shaking and silent laughter drained the last bit of hope I had in my medical barber.

"I'm sorry," he said, wiping his eyes but still laughing—so really, how sorry could he be? "It's just that you think you've seen everything, and then . . ." He couldn't finish. He excused himself for a moment, and I heard what sounded like sneezing laughter going on outside the closed door.

It was a good thing Sunny was busy playing doctor right now because if she were here with me, I'd glue this hospital pillow right to her butt! Instead, I stuck the thin, scratchy pillow up to my face and shouted into it, "Sunny Sweet is going to be sooo sorry!" Silly, maybe, but it made me feel better so I did it again. *"Sunny Sweet, you are going to be sooo sooorry!"*

The medical barber walked back in, and this time he was ready for business. He put down his bag and turned on the light over my bed, focusing it on top of my head. It burned my scalp a little, but I didn't say anything. I wanted him to be able to get a good, long look at what he was dealing with.

"Hmm," he said. "She used a cold-setting epoxy."

I didn't say anything. I didn't really care what materials the shrinky-dink snake used. But I was starting to like my medical barber more. The word "epoxy" made him sound official and smart, which meant that any minute he was going to pull a prescription out of his bag and remove this nightmare forever.

"Is this a peanut?" he said, picking something out of my hair.

I bit my lip. I didn't want to tell him about the freezer or how my mom thought that since peanut butter was supposed to get gum out of your hair that it would somehow also remove fake flowers.

He sniffed. "She must have mixed the epoxy with peanut butter," he whispered, "but that doesn't make any sense."

I sat with my mouth shut while he picked out a few more peanuts and examined them. He messed around with the flowers for fifteen minutes. Just when I was beginning to feel like a glass vase being arranged, my medical barber stood back and looked at me.

"What?" I asked.

"It looks like your sister used a thermosetting resin," he said, looking serious, "which is character- ized by monomeric units that are linked together by

64

chemical bonds and form three-dimensional net-
works that are infusible and insoluble."

All of a sudden I didn't like my medical barber
anymore.

"What?" I asked.

"This stuff is not coming out," he said, giving a
little shake of his head.

And I wished more than anything that I did have Calvin's disease, because then at least I could be dying right now!

"How am I supposed to live like this?" I cried.

"You don't," said my medical barber, although I was beginning to suspect that he might just be a regular barber who happened to know a weird amount about glue.

"What?" I asked.

"We'll have to shave your head," he said.

"WHAT!" I shouted.

"We'll have to . . ."

I fell back onto the hospital bed and waved my hand at him to stop. I had heard him. I was just shouting to shout.

My hair? He couldn't take my hair! I had been growing my hair for as long as I could remember. And maybe no one ever paid attention to me at school unless they needed to look at my homework, and maybe I didn't really have, you know, one particular *best* friend. But I had hair! And it was nice hair. Everybody said how nice my hair was. In fact, the only time

Alex and Nicole ever talked to me was about my hair. The first month after we moved here, Alex and Nicole and I were in the girls' bathroom together. Nicole took her brush and started brushing my hair. While she brushed, she said things like "Your hair is so beautiful" and "What a pretty dark color it is" and "It is so thick," and her words, just like her hairbrush in my hair, made my skin tingle with happiness. I had beautiful hair. I *had* beautiful hair. And now I would be what? I couldn't even think that word!

"Listen," my medical barber said, looking down at my chart, "Marsha . . ."

"Masha," I corrected into the bed sheets.

"I know that hair is important. And I'm truly sorry. But there is no way to get these out of your hair without shaving them off."

His "explanation" wasn't making me feel any better.

"Let's get in touch with your parents," he said.

"I just have a mom," I blubbered, because I was sobbing now like a big fat baby.

"Let's give your mom a call," he said.

"No," I said, sitting up.

"Okay, listen," he said, looking back at me. "Let me take a sample of the glue down to the lab and have it checked out."

"Because you think that maybe you'll come up with another idea to get this off?" I asked, sitting up a little straighter in the bed.

He looked at me with a long frown. Then he opened up his bag and pulled out a pair of scissors. Leaning over, he snipped off a small lock of my hair close to my scalp. "Don't get your hopes up," he said. And then he turned and left the room.

Getting a Break

The door hadn't even finished closing before I hopped off the bed. The freaky little hobbit doctor could stay and finish her rounds, but I was getting out of here.

Walking out the door seemed too risky. I ran to the window. It looked out onto the roof of another part of the hospital. It seemed to be about a twenty-foot drop. I wondered if I hung down by my fingertips how many feet less the fall would be. I might break a leg or something, but I'd pretty much survive. I thought about the guy in the ER with his leg in a cast, and then I imagined Nicole and Alex begging me to let them carry my books through the halls of school. I searched for a way to open the window, but it had no opening. How could this be? Wasn't this a fire hazard? What would happen if there was an emergency and I needed to get out?

I eyed the room for some sort of tool. There was the bed, a chair, and a bunch of cabinets. I opened up the cabinets, not knowing exactly what I was looking for. Maybe a screwdriver? Or a window-opening tool? All I found were shelves filled with medical stuff like cotton balls and plastic gloves. I spotted a box filled with big Popsicle sticks and plucked one out. Not sure how I might use it to open the window, I decided to stick it in my mouth. I scooted over to the mirror on the wall and opened wide, saying, "Ahhhhh." My tonsils danced in the back of my throat. I did it again, but it wasn't that exciting the second time. Plus the wood taste of the stick got kind of gross.

I tossed the stick into the little garbage can and pulled out a couple of the plastic gloves. Maybe I could put them on and punch my fist through the

70

glass so I wouldn't get cut. They were harder to get on than they looked. I got two fingers into one of them and then gave up. I'd always wanted to blow these gloves up like you see in the movies. I put my mouth to the wrist part of the glove and blew, but I ended up with a mouth full of dusty powder that made me just about gag. I threw them both in the garbage with the Popsicle stick, rinsed my mouth in the tiny sink, and moved on to the next cabinet. It was filled with bandages, and each shelf was marked with the word "sterilized" across it, which made me want to pull everything out and touch it all, but I didn't. I closed it up and opened the last cabinet. It was empty. Bummer.

I heard voices outside my door, and I froze. The voices moved on down the hall and finally faded away.

This was getting me absolutely nowhere. I wasn't going to find a screwdriver, I wasn't going to jump out the window, and I wasn't going to leave Sunny and Mrs. Song. I was trapped.

I stared at the door. It had been about fifteen minutes since my medical barber had left. He was bound to be back soon. Was I really going to sit here and let him shave my head? I grabbed my hair with both hands. No way! I had to act.

I swiped Mrs. Song's hat from the bed and crunched it down over my head, tying the ribbons under my chin. Then I tiptoed to the door and pulled it open two inches, sticking my nose out. I could hear voices and beeping and ringing of phones and stuff, but I didn't see any people. I reached down and stretched the bracelet that the nurses had put on me when I almost had Calvin's disease until I could pull it off. Then I stepped forward, letting my hospital room door close behind me with a soft click.

I was out.

I didn't exactly have a fully formed plan, but I felt weirdly excited, like this was the first time today that I was in charge. I was the one who decided to leave my hospital room. I was the one who decided to walk down the hall . . . to turn the corner . . . to nod politely at a passing person even though my heart was beating so loud my ears throbbed.

I knew that I had to find Sunny, so I started poking my head into random rooms. Mostly the people in the beds didn't even look up. They were sleeping or reading or watching their TVs. A nurse passed me in the hall, and I held my breath. "Out for a stroll?" she asked. I nodded.

I checked all the rooms on one hall and then started down the next. She could be anywhere. I tried to think what kind of doctor the nurse said Sunny was following. It started with an *O*. I couldn't remember.

I passed by a nurses' station and tried to look normal.

"Can I help you?" asked a lady behind the desk.

"I'm just out for a stroll," I said, using the nurse's line.

She gave me a big smile and a nod. It worked!

The hospital halls seemed to make a square, and I followed around it, looking and listening for any sign of Sunny. She wasn't anywhere. I thought about going back to the front desk but didn't want to risk bumping into my medical barber. Why, why, why did Sunny have to go and follow this doctor around? Why couldn't she have just stayed in her room and eaten crackers like me?

I decided to try another floor. I clomped down the staircase. There were lots of people on this floor, and no one stopped to notice me. There were also a million rooms. Most of them had closed doors, and I was too scared to open them. I walked slowly up and down the halls, trying to see if I could hear Sunny behind any of the doors. If only I knew what that doctor that she was following did. Wait. It had something to do with bones.

I walked up to the first desk I saw. There was a girl sitting in her chair picking at her nails with a paper clip. "What kind of doctor helps your bones?" I asked.

She looked up at me and just stared.

"I'm . . . I'm doing a report at school," I told her.

"An orthopedist," she said, going back to her nails. "The orthopedics department is on the sixth floor, west wing."

"Thanks," I said.

I got to the sixth floor easily enough, but finding the west wing was another problem. It took me ten minutes to locate it on the map and then another ten to walk over to it. I wandered around the west wing, checking in any door that was open. This floor wasn't as crowded, and a couple of people asked if they could help me. I used my line "I'm just out for a stroll," and they let me be. Some people did give me questioning looks, but this could have been because I was starting to sweat buckets. Where was my little sister? On my third trip around the same hallway, I officially began to freak out.

I decided to go back and search the east wing. This plan seemed better than no plan at all, and I headed back. A door was open that had been closed before, so I poked my head in.

It was a small waiting room. Against the back of the room was a giant fish tank filled with all kinds of colorful fish, plastic, swaying seaweed, and little toy reefs and shells. I walked over to the tank and leaned my tired head against the glass. It was nice to watch the fish instead of searching endlessly for Sunny. There were a bunch of long, skinny fish that stuck together in a little herd. There was one flat-looking, ugly brown fish with long whiskers like a cat that stayed at the bottom by the colorful stones. But mostly the tank was filled with these blue-and-yellow fish that looked like they were a big family of cousins or something. They kind of darted around in the water as if they were playing a game with each other. Watching the sluggish flat fish and the twitchy little skinny fish and all the pretty swooshing of the blue-and-yellow fish made me feel like this whole day wasn't happening. I started to relax with the quiet swimming of fish. But then I caught my reflection in the glass of the tank. And there I was, standing all by myself with Mrs. Song's hat on and my head still full of flowers.

All of a sudden being in charge didn't feel so good. My escape from the hospital room, the killer virus, Mrs. Song being sick, not knowing where the heck Sunny was . . . it all felt wrong. I wanted to be home in my own house. If only I could find Sunny.

I called to her in my head, "Sunny, where are you?"

I would do just about anything to see her spooky little face, stringy blond hair, and skinny arms and legs standing in front of me.

I felt a little dizzy, and tired.

As I slid into a chair next to the tank, a door opened up, making me jump back up. A nurse stuck her head into the room, spotted me, and smiled brightly. "Hi," she said.

My heart shook. I tried to smile back, but my mouth pulled itself down into a frown and all of a sudden I was struggling to hold back tears.

"Maria?" she asked.

"Masha," I whispered.

"Why don't you come on in now," she said, opening the door wide and waving me in.

I didn't move.

She looked at me and sighed like she completely understood everything that I was going through. Then she let go of the door and walked toward me. "It's all going to be okay," she said, looking right into my eyes. And I believed her. Then she added, "I was just on the phone with your mom and . . ."

The mention of my mom opened a tiny crack in my heart, and tears popped out onto the ledges of my eyes. Noticing, the nurse rushed to my side and put her arm gently around my shoulder, making the whole thing worse. "Oh, baby, it's going to be okay," she said as she led me through the door. "It won't hurt nearly as bad as breaking it did. Trust me, I've done this a hundred times."

"Breaking what?" I sniffed through a few of the falling tears.

"Now, come on," she said, smiling at me. "It won't be that bad, trust me."

"What won't be that bad?"

She sat me down on a long, hard, platformlike bed with a scratchy paper sheet on it and walked over to her supply cabinets. Another door opened and a second nurse walked in. He grunted a "hi" to the nice nurse and then glanced my way with a half smile. When his eyes landed on my hat, he stopped short, his white sneakers squeaking on the hospital floor. His face gave a twitch. I was sure that he was going to ask why I was wearing this ridiculous hat, but then the moment was gone and he headed over to a flat screen on the wall. I guess I wasn't that interesting. He shoved a group of black papers onto the screen one at a time, and then flipped a switch. The black papers lit up. They were X-rays of the glowing white bones of an arm. And it was broken. Twice.

"Um," I gulped, sitting up and cradling my poor broken arm against my chest.

The nurse walked over to me. "Hi, Maria," he said, opening up a chart.

"Masha," I said, "but I think . . ."

"Is your birthday March 7?" he asked.

"No, but that's my sister's birthday," I said, which it was.

He rolled his eyes and then looked down at my wrist, I guess for that bracelet I had taken off.

"She doesn't have her ID bracelet," he said over his shoulder to the nice nurse. His voice was loud, and it felt like it bounced off my chest.

"I pulled it off," I whispered.

The nice nurse turned from collecting her stuff and walked over to us, looking at the mean nurse but really talking to me. "Maria is pretty nervous and in pain. It's not every day that you break your arm. She doesn't want to be here, and I understand that." Then she smiled at me as if to say, ignore this guy, he doesn't get us.

"Um, I, you, have the wrong person. I didn't break my arm. I was just looking at the fish."

"She took the splint off?" the mean nurse questioned. He reached for my left arm and I pulled it away, hugging it to my chest.

The nice nurse glared at the back of the mean nurse's head and rolled over a chair next to me, sitting down so her face was even with my face. Then she looked into my eyes, so sweet and kind, and my eyes filled with tears again. She put her hand on my leg. "Okay, honey, we realize that this day has been a real tough one for you." I nodded and a couple of big, salty drips plopped onto my thighs. "But," she continued, "it's all going to be fine now. We are going to take care of everything from here on out, okay?"

"Okay," I whispered.

"Anyway," she said, grinning and reaching into her supplies and pulling out a book, "this is the fun part." She opened the book and started flipping through the pages, holding them for me to see. They were filled with different squares of colors. "What is your favorite color?" she asked.

I shrugged.

"Green? Blue?" She kept turning the pages. "Orange?"

"Orange," I said. Sunny was right. My favorite color was orange. Sunny was always right.

"Orange it is," she said, snapping the book closed and smiling. I smiled back.

In the corner of my eye, I could see the mean nurse's long face, but I tried to focus on my nice nurse. She told me to lie down and relax, which I did. Then she started talking about how great the cast was going to be. How I was going to be able to swim and take showers and how everybody was going to be able to sign it.

I lay on the scratchy paper, shaking. Was I really about to get a cast . . . a real cast? I couldn't believe it. I had wished for one for so long and here I was getting it, just like that. I wiped my face with my good arm and sniffed. All my sad thoughts from the fish tank disappeared and were replaced with visions of me walking into school with my new broken arm. And since I had broken my arm in two places, I bet that it was going to be one of those really good casts where it included your elbow and went all the way down over your hand so you couldn't even use a pencil. From the glowing-white pictures, it looked like I had broken my left arm and I actually wrote with my right hand, but still, who cares because I was getting a cast! A giant white—no, wait—a giant orange cast! Then I remembered that you don't get to walk on crutches if you have a broken arm and my happiness dimmed for a second, but only for a second because, duh, a cast was a cast! Everybody was going to be able to sign it. And everybody included Nicole and Alex.

"Will the names come off if I get the cast wet?" I asked, a little worried.

The nurse stopped prepping my arm and smiled. "That is the best part. If you use a permanent marker, you can have all your friends sign your cast and the ink won't come off in the bath or shower. So you can scrub-a-dub-dub and all those signatures will stay right in place."

"Really?"

"Really."

"That is so cool." I giggled.

She gently wrapped a rubbery bandage around my arm, from my wrist to my elbow, and then got out a roll of long, thin cotton. "See," she said, breathing lightly on my arm, "this isn't such a bad day after all. Right?" she asked, winding the cotton around the bandage.

"No," I agreed. "Maybe not."

The mean nurse hovered in the background.

"Nice hat," he said.

I ignored him.

Dr. Sonya Sweet

My cast was *awesometastic*! It was bright orange and went all the way from almost my shoulder down to my hand, just like I hoped it would. It was thick and hard and just so, so *real*. I have a broken arm! I broke my arm in two places! I can't wait to get out in the world and show everybody.

Shawna got done casting it in fifteen minutes. That was the nice nurse's name, Shawna. And she wasn't really a nurse, but a resident. That meant she was pretty much almost a doctor. She was putting my cast in a big blue sling when there was a light knock on the door.

"Come on in," Shawna sang.

The door opened and in walked a small woman in a white coat followed by an even smaller figure in a white coat . . . Sunny Sweet!

My body jolted, and I slipped off the bed.

"Whoa," Shawna laughed, catching me. "It's only Dr. Dorney. She's the attending physician, so she's

going to take a quick look at my work and then you're on your way home."

Sunny and I stared at each other while the doctor and Shawna said hello and began to talk about my arm, or rather, Maria's arm.

Oh my gosh, I just stole someone's broken arm!

Dr. Dorney introduced Sunny to Shawna and me as her "little assistant," and Shawna introduced me to the doctor. I think I said hello, but I couldn't take my eyes off Sunny. Neither of us knew what to do. Sunny recovered before I did.

"How did you break your arm, Maria?" she asked. I could see the corners of her tiny mouth holding back a smile.

"My little sister pushed me in front of a car," I said.

Shawna and the doctor gasped.

"Just joking," I mumbled.

The doctor called Sunny over to see "my" X-rays. I tried to escape by telling Shawna that I had to use the bathroom.

"Let's wait until the doctor is finished," Shawna said.

"I see she broke both her ulna and her radius," Sunny said. Turning to me, she added, "You must be in a lot of pain, Maria."

"I'm fine." I coughed.

The doctor picked up my chart from the small desk by the X-ray board. "It's been about three hours since you came through the ER, Maria," she said to me. And then she turned to Shawna. "Have you given her anything for the pain, Shawna?"

"I don't need anything," I told them. "I feel super great."

"I've read a lot about pain management," Sunny said. "Isn't it best to keep on a steady dosage to keep the pain from returning, Dr. Dorney?"

The doctor looked at Sunny like she was one of the Seven Wonders of the World instead of the freak of nature that she was. "I think that Dr. Sonya Sweet is correct," said the doctor.

"I'm on it," said Shawna, coming at me with a needle.

"No!" was all I got out before she stuck me in my good arm.

My mouth fell open, and I looked over at Sunny. She backed away a little and giggled.

"That will take care of the pain for a while," said the doctor, "although it may make you a little sleepy."

A warm feeling ran through me like someone had covered me in a soft, cozy blanket. Shawna rolled a wheelchair into the room, and the doctor and Shawna helped me into it. Shawna then wheeled me back out into the waiting room. I tried to catch Sunny's eye, but she was busy playing with a piece of X-ray equipment. I guess the joy of poisoning her sister didn't last as long as the actual poison did.

Shawna positioned me next to the fish tank. "I will be right back," she said. I waited for Sunny to follow me out of the room, but she didn't. After staring at the closed door between Sunny and me for five minutes, I began to forget why I cared whether Sunny came through it or not. My cast sat in my lap. I ran my hand lovingly over it. It was still a little wet, but Shawna said it would dry in about half an hour. At least I still had my cast. It was so orange, and I mean really orange.

The swimming fish caught my attention. I watched

them until my eyes started to water, then I let out a giant yawn. Sunny once told me that scientists learned that animals were attracted to certain colors, and that sharks were attracted to the color orange. I made a note in my head that I better not go swimming in the ocean in the next six weeks. That is how long Shawna said I would get to wear it. Six whole weeks.

To test the shark theory, I clunked my cast up against the glass of the fish tank to see if any of the fish noticed. Before I could tell if they liked the color orange, I was interrupted by a lady walking into the waiting room, followed by a girl my age with her arm in a splint and a blue sling just like mine. The girl looked pale and was moaning, and the lady seemed a little angry. She glanced around the room, and then with a sigh sank into one of the seats. The girl sat down next to her. She sniffed a couple of times and then started moaning again. I knew exactly who they were: Maria, who was born the same day of the year as Sunny, and her mother. I slid down into my wheelchair.

"Look at that brave little girl," the mother said to Maria, motioning over to me. "She isn't whining about her arm." The mother gave me a tight smile. "And her arm looks like it's been broken much worse than yours."

I choked on a breath of air that was trying to get down into my lungs. And then I couldn't stop coughing. It sounded like I was coughing inside a tin can.

I needed to get out of here. I tried to wheel my chair with my good arm, but all I did was turn myself in a semicircle so I totally faced Maria and her mother.

Maria glanced up at me. I could tell she wished I would disappear in a puff of smoke. I kind of wished I would too. Maybe she somehow knew that this was actually her broken arm I was wearing.

Somewhere inside my head a voice was shouting at me to get out of there, but that voice

91

didn't seem to have control over my legs. Weirdly, I wanted to close my eyes and take a nap, even though I knew that if Shawna came through that door and saw Maria and her mother, I was going to be in huge, huge trouble.

The door opened, and out walked Shawna with juice and crackers in her hand for me. She looked over at Maria and her mother. "I'll be with you in just a moment," she said. She put the crackers in my lap and tried to hand me the juice, but my arm wouldn't move from the arm of the wheelchair. I blinked at Shawna, waiting for her to realize what was happening, when there was a pinging of a few notes over a sound system followed by a woman's soft voice, *"Code yellow, department 66, room 452. Code yellow. Code yellow, department 66, room 452. Code yellow."*

Shawna stood next to me until the woman over the sound system had repeated the message. Then she put my juice next to the fish tank, gave my head a quick pat, and hurried from the room.

I swallowed a giant breath of air, and relief washed over me.

Once again the pinging sounded overhead. "Great, another one," I thought. Hopefully this would keep everyone busy until I could figure out how to use my legs again and I could get out of here.

The same female voice came back over the sound system. *"Would Marsha Sweet please come to the front desk on the main floor of the Shapiro Building? Marsha Sweet, please come to the front desk on the main floor of the Shapiro Building."*

My face flushed red, and I started to sweat. I looked over at Maria and her mother, but of course they just looked back at me. They didn't know that I was "Marsha."

The door opened again. I closed my eyes and waited for the world to end.

"Let's get out of here," whispered a voice that wasn't Shawna's.

I opened my eyes.

Sunny.

I'd never been so happy to see my little sister in all my life!

The Fix

Sunny pushed me out the door and away from poor Maria and her mean mother. We headed down a hallway, and then we made a right and headed down another. My neck felt like a rubber band, and every time I blinked I had to pull my eyelids back open again.

"Where are we going?" I mumbled.

"Don't worry," Sunny said, "no place bad."

"I wasn't worried until you said *that*!" I said.

A lady with a plastic name tag swinging on a string around her neck walked toward us. She slowed her high-heeled step as we approached each other. "We're just out for a stroll," I said, as a tiny bit of drool made its way over my lip and down my chin. And then I yawned so wide and long that my jaw just about cracked in two. When the yawn was finally over, the lady was gone and we were sitting in front of a row of elevators.

Again, the soft notes played over the sound system, followed by the lady's voice. *"Would Marsha Sweet please come to the front desk on the main floor of the Shapiro Building? Marsha Sweet, please come to the front desk on the main floor of the Shapiro Building."*

"Th-they're afterrr usss," I slurred, closing my eyes and leaning my head back in my wheelchair. I wanted to care that they were after us, but I was just so tired.

"Don't worry. I'm going to fix everything."

"Nooo!" I shouted, but only in my dreams. Because I was now definitely, mostly, and unfortunately asleee . . .

* * *

"It pinches," I said.

"I'm fixing it," said Sunny as she loosened the strap on my helmet.

"I don't want to go," I whined.

"Stop complaining," my mother said. "Just think—you're going to be the very first fifth grader in space! What a special gift your little sister is giving you."

Sunny strapped me down into her rocket and then lit a fiery torch. "Good-bye, *Marsha*," she said, smiling.

"Nooo!"

I sat up, sucking in a giant gulp of air like I'd just come up after a really deep dive into a pool. I wasn't in a rocket. I wasn't blasting off from Earth. I wasn't exploding into a million pieces.

It was a dream . . . just a dream. I laughed out loud—the sound of my laughter bouncing off the walls and coming back at me. I was alone in a dark room lying on a hard bed. Where was I? Maybe this was a dream too.

The door opened, and Sunny peeked in.

"You're awake," she said.

"Where are we?"

"The basement of the hospital," she said.

"Huh?" I scooted off the bed, noticing the cast on my arm. And then it all came back to me—Mrs. Song on the bike, the ambulance, Calvin, my arm, the lady on the loudspeaker, and Sunny wheeling me away.

I stared hard at Sunny. She had that look.

"What did you do?"

"Now, don't be mad, Masha," she said, taking a step backward.

"Sunny . . . what did you do?" My hands flew to my head. I felt hair. I felt flowers. I felt itchy and damp. I felt nothing different.

"You didn't do anything?"

"I couldn't dissolve the glue," she said, her skinny little shoulders falling an inch. "I tried, Masha, I really did." She stepped all the way through the door, holding her hands behind her back.

"What's behind your back?"

"Nothing," she said.

"Sunny," I growled.

She glanced over her shoulder. "It's just a simple pair of levers hinged at the fulcrum," she said.

"Sunny," I demanded, "what is in your hands?"

She pulled out a large pair of scissors.

"Sunny!"

My shout made her drop the scissors. "I was going to try to cut them off. You weren't even going to notice."

"I would have killed you," I said. "Let's go." I grabbed her by the elbow. The sleep had felt good and I was no longer groggy. "We're getting out of here."

"What about Mrs. Song?"

"We're going to go down and get Mrs. Song and then we're going home. Where's Mrs. Song's hat?"

Sunny handed me the hat from off the counter, and I looked around the room for a mirror. There was none, so I stepped in front of a small, silver paper-towel dispenser pinned to the wall over the sink to see myself and pulled Mrs. Song's hat on. And then I yanked it off with a scream.

"Sunny Sweet! What did you do?"

"I told you not to get mad," Sunny said.

"Why is my hair green?"

"Well, first I tried acetone, but that didn't work. So I found bleach, thinking that—"

"Stop!" I said. "I don't need to hear about your evil scientific methods."

I gazed into the towel dispenser. My hair was shamrock-shake green.

I turned to Sunny. "You have to fix this!"

She picked up the scissors.

"Not like that."

"Masha, let me cut them out and then we can dye your hair back to brown. You'll never be able to tell this even happened."

I looked back into the paper-towel dispenser. A giant leprechaun looked back. "Okay," I said, giving up. I slowly climbed back onto the bed that I'd woken up on.

Smiling, Sunny dragged a stool over to the table and switched on a light over my head. Her skinny little arms loomed in front of my face and I could hear her short, excited breaths in my ear. Her fingers filtered through my hair and I felt her choose a flower. There was a glint of metal from the scissors as they moved toward my head, a moment of silence, and then there was the horrible crunching of scissors meeting, and slicing through, hair. And then there was a tiny sting. "Whoops," said Sunny.

"Ouch!" My hand flew to my head, forgetting that it had a heavy cast attached to it. The weight of the cast made me lose control of the speed of my arm, and it socked me right in my eye, hard. Silver sparks floated inches from my pupils . . . or in my pupils, I couldn't tell which, and I slid down onto the bed with a moan.

When I turned my head, I saw a tiny bit of blood on my hand. My blood!

I jumped up, my head spinning, and clomped like Frankenstein's monster over to the paper-towel dispenser. My mouth fell open. "Ahhh," I howled. I now had a huge bald spot on the top right side of my head, along with a small cut by my scalp, and worst of all, a very fast-forming black eye!

I was a monster. I was Sunny's monster.

"It's a very small avulsion," Sunny said. "Let me try again. I promise not to cut you this time. Let's call that strike one."

I didn't answer. I gazed into that silver dispenser at myself in horror.

"That's a sports metaphor," Sunny said. "Strike

one." Like I cared about sports after what she had just done to me.

"This can't get worse," I whispered.

"Maybe it can," said Sunny. "They keep calling you over the loudspeaker. I'm pretty sure security is searching for you."

I sighed and rolled my head back, looking up at the ceiling.

"Let's just go home, Masha," she said. "We can take the bus. I can look up the bus number right now. And we can call Mrs. Song and tell her we're going home."

"You've had your cell phone with you the whole time?"

"I always have my cell phone," she said.

I leaned against the table and ran my fingers lightly under my throbbing eye, wiping away the tears. I knew that I had only one hope left, and that was my medical barber.

"No, Sunny, we're not going home. We're going to the front desk on the main floor of the Shapiro Building, and I'm going to face the music."

"Facing the music was what soldiers did when they were being dishonorably discharged from the army," Sunny said. "They would play drums at the discharge ceremony and make the dishonored soldiers walk past them. Are we discharging ourselves?" she asked, her giant blue eyes blinking up at me.

"No," I told her. "We're checking in."

Being Marsha Sweet

Enough was enough. I had ten different shades of daisies glued to my head, green hair, my arm in an orange cast, and a black eye. I was like some crazy nightmare rainbow.

I put Mrs. Song's hat back over my head and crammed tissues into the side of it to stop the bleeding from where Sunny nicked me. And then I marched us down the hallway, following the signs to the Shapiro Building. We crossed over a little bridge that took us above a street and past a bunch of people. Nobody stopped us, but some of them followed us with their eyes as we passed.

Once we got to the Shapiro Building, finding the main lobby was easy, but crossing the expanse of brown-tiled floor to the giant desk in the center wasn't. I froze about twenty-five feet out. I swear I could hear those drums that Sunny talked about pounding inside my head.

"What?" asked Sunny, stopping alongside me. "Do you want to run?"

I did want to run. But I knew that I couldn't. My feet started walking toward the desk even as a voice deep in my flowered skull shouted, "No, no, no!"

Sunny grabbed my hand and held me back. "Come on, Masha, the door is right there."

I looked over to where she was motioning. I could see the blue sky and the trees outside the front of the hospital. It was weird that today was still today. It felt like we'd been running around this hospital for three weeks.

"Let's just leave," Sunny begged. "The bus stop is right out front—I checked."

"You can't go around doing whatever you want, Sunny. You have to follow the rules sometimes," I told her.

"I do follow the rules. I'm following the rules of gravity right now. You don't see me floating around in this lobby, do you?"

I rolled my eyes. I never knew what she was talking about. I started toward the front desk again.

"Wait!" Sunny whispered, holding my arm. "I know I can figure out how to get the glue to dissolve once we get home, Masha."

I looked down at her. I so wanted to believe her. She got excited. She had me. "All I need is my chem set C3000, and . . ."

"Forget it, Sunny. I'm not a gerbil. I'm, I'm *Marsha Sweet*," I said, and I stomped up to the front desk.

There was a small, older lady behind the desk in what looked like a flight attendant dress. "Can I help you?" she asked.

"Hi, I'm Marsha Sweet."

She looked at me for a second and then picked up

the phone. "Security? Yes, it's Thelma from Shapiro Main. I have Marsha Sweet here with me."

She listened for a second and then hung up. "Someone will be right down," she said. Then she noticed Sunny, and she smiled brightly. "Would the little girl like a lollipop? I have eight different flavors."

Sunny jumped up and down in front of the desk as if she were just a sweet little kid who would love a lollipop. I wanted a lollipop too, but she didn't ask me.

Someone was right down. Before Sunny chose one of the eight flavored lollipops, my medical barber and a security guard came hurrying into the lobby.

"Where have you been?" he asked. And then he stopped and stared at me, his mouth hanging open. "What happened?"

"My little sister happened," I said, pointing at Sunny. Sunny grinned at him from behind her lollipop. And then she began to skip around the lobby, sucking on her candy and humming and generally doing an excellent impression of an innocent six-year-old.

"She broke your arm?" he asked.

"Oh, never mind." I groaned. "Did the lab find something to get these flowers out with?"

"My gosh—and your eye?"

"It was always like this. You probably didn't notice before because you were really busy laughing at all the plastic flowers glued to my head!"

I could see that he suddenly felt guilty. Sometimes adults were pretty easy to handle.

"Anyway," I said, trying to make him focus on what was really the problem here—my head. "Did the lab find something to get these off with?" My chest swelled with hope as the words left my mouth.

"Jim, can you radio for an orderly?" my medical barber asked the security guard. "We need someone to take Marsha to pediatrics."

Jim spoke into his radio, and I waited for an answer.

My medical barber avoided my eyes. "Let's just get you to pediatrics so we can take care of things."

"Does taking care of things mean that I get to keep my hair?" Green or not, I still wanted it on my head.

"I'm sorry, Marsha," he said, finally looking at me.

My eyes stung from held-back tears as I looked over at Sunny rolling around on a couch across the lobby, busily sucking her lollipop. Just then, an old, bent man in white walked into the lobby pushing a wheelchair.

The orderly.

Now there was nothing I could do to stop the tears from sliding down my cheeks, and not because I was right back where I was before I became a freakish monster, but because the orderly was totally and completely . . . bald!

Rolling toward Freakdom

W hy can't I just walk?" I asked.

"This here is the way we do things," said the old bald guy, frowning. I settled into the chair.

"Can I ride in it with you?" asked Sunny, skipping over.

"No," I said.

"Is this the little florist?" asked my medical barber.

"Very funny," I said.

"That was some glue you mixed up," he said to Sunny. "The lab is examining it now."

"I blended cyanoacrylate with amorphous silica," she said.

"How did you deal with solubility?"

"I heated it." She smiled.

My medical barber shook his head, clearly impressed with Sunny's skills at ruining my life.

"Come on," he said to Sunny. "Let's take a trip downstairs to the lab." And then remembering that there was someone attached to the glue, he turned to me and said, "I'll meet you in pediatrics in a few minutes."

He walked off, chattering to my little sister like her stinking best buddy. I opened my mouth to say something. Something like, "I am a person, not a science experiment," but between the wheelchair I didn't need, a black eye, orange cast, and green hair, I really was a science experiment.

My medical barber turned back to me before leaving the lobby. "Don't go running off again," he called.

I gave a vague nod. This lab rat was going to keep her options open.

* * *

112

The old bald guy wheeled me down a hundred hall-ways, and I swear we turned the same corner, like, ten times. We finally ended up at a long line of elevators where we sat for about an hour because he never pushed the button. I guess I could have told him, but it wasn't like I was in any hurry to get anywhere. And it didn't seem like he was either.

The elevator doors finally opened, and we rolled inside. Just after the doors shut behind us, I heard the old bald guy sniff a couple of times.

"It's peanut butter," I said. "We thought it would help get the flowers out."

"How'd they get in there?" he asked.

"My sister glued them to my head while I was sleeping."

It's funny how just saying those words could get my blood boiling just as much as they had when I first starting saying them. I glanced up at the old man with his bald head shining in the overhead lights of the elevator. That is what I will look like in less than an hour. I couldn't take my eyes off the round smoothness of it.

The old man noticed me looking at him. "See this here scar?" he asked, pointing to a two-inch scar along his chin. "My brother did this to me when we was kids. He was swinging a stick around like some kind of sword. He told me to pretend I was a dragon. Well, I barely breathed a lick of fire and *whack*, he hit me with the stick. It took sixteen stitches to close it up."

"They have to shave my head," I said.

"Tough one," he said.

Pediatrics was louder and more crowded than any of the other millions of hallways that the bald guy and I had been rolling around on.

Peeking into the rooms as we passed, I saw kids of all ages in beds and wheelchairs. Some seemed to be held together by metal and others had gauze wrapped around their legs or arms, and all of them had the bubble bags like Mrs. Song's attached to them on rolling sticks. It was as if I had just been wheeled into the X-Men mansion, only these were X-kids and I wondered what each of their superhero powers were.

"Where do I put her?" the bald guy asked the nurse behind the front desk.

"Hi, honey," the nurse said to me with a sad smile. "You the one with those plastic flowers stuck to your head?" It's a question that you can't imagine anyone ever asking you.

"Yes," I answered.

"Just set her here next to me, Al. We don't have any open rooms right now." And then, like I didn't just hear her talk to Al, she glanced over at me and said, "You get to be special and sit right here by me and keep me company for a while. How does that sound?"

"That sounds great," I said, even though I could tell that she wasn't really asking me the question. I was going to be keeping her company even though I didn't want to. What I really wanted was my own room with a TV and crackers and orange juice, and to be withering away from Calvin's disease. But you don't get everything you want in life.

The nurse went back to work, and I realized that "keeping her company" meant just sitting in this wheelchair next to her while she went about her business.

At first I could feel the eyes of nurses and people looking at me as they passed by, but a girl in a wheelchair with a black eye and a broken arm wearing a funny hat doesn't seem to be that interesting in a place like this. In the ten minutes that I had been sitting here, I had seen a kid wheeled by in his bed with his entire body inside a cast and another girl with a

116

steel bolt going through one of her knees. Soon every-thing in the hall was business as usual and no one noticed me, and I got a little lonely. But then I felt someone still noticing.

She was maybe about my age, and was sitting in a wheelchair too, just like me. Although she wasn't just like me in that she was hunched over a little, like her spine wasn't able to hold her completely up, making her head and neck kind of smushed closer to her legs. She had one of those bubble bags attached to a rolling stick next to her.

I didn't want to keep looking at her, but she kept looking at me. So I looked back. Her hair was in a ponytail held by a blue hair tie. Her eyes were round and dark. I smiled. She didn't smile back. I looked away.

I wondered what made her hunched like that. I wondered if it hurt. I wondered if her legs worked. And then my medical barber showed up and reminded me why I was sitting in the hallway of a hospital.

"Hi, Sue," he said to the nurse at the desk. "Have you been watering my patient for me?"

117

They laughed.

I didn't think it was that funny.

"Have you gotten in touch with her mother?" he asked.

She smiled over at me. "No. According to the chart from upstairs, her mother isn't home and Marsha can't remember the correct work or cell phone numbers."

"My name is Masha," I said.

They both smiled at me, but neither of them actually looked directly at me.

"Where's my little sister?" I asked.

"She's demonstrating her process to the lab," he said.

"But I thought there was no way to get it off me."

"There isn't, but the guys in the lab were really interested in how she made the glue."

Great! I was stuck here in a wheelchair about to get my head shaved while Sunny was busy playing real, live evil scientist.

"Anyway," continued my medical barber, "the lab found traces of the chemical styrene in the glue, and we need to get those flowers removed as soon as possible."

"Wait!" I said. They both really looked at me this time. "You're going to do this without my mother's permission?"

The nurse stood up. "Sweetheart," she said, bending over me and staring me right in the eyes just the way Shawna had done, "we would really love to wait for your mother, and normally we would because . . ." I didn't hear what she said next. Behind the nurse I could see the girl in the wheelchair with the blue hair tie watching me, and all of a sudden I felt ashamed. This girl obviously had some pretty serious trouble, much worse than a headful of plastic flowers. And it wasn't just her; it was every kid on this floor, and Mrs. Song, and even poor Calvin. I'm not saying that getting your head shaved is no big deal. I mean, truthfully, I could barely keep myself from sliding to the floor screaming, but when you're looking into the face of someone whose spine doesn't seem to be working all that well, I don't know, I guess it helps you buck up. Or maybe it *makes* you buck up.

"That's fine," I said, "shave away," and I waved my hand in the air like my medical barber and Nurse Sue had just asked if they could cut ahead of me in the lunch line on a Tuesday for Tuna Surprise (which is this square piece of fish that smells like cat food). Although I did gulp pretty hard after I finished saying it and hoped that Nurse Sue, my medical barber, and the girl in the wheelchair didn't hear it.

Embracing Your Freakdom

S̲o̲ where can I do this?" asked the medical barber, looking up and down the hall.

Nurse Sue thought for a few seconds.

"How about in the rec room?" suggested the girl in the wheelchair.

"Good idea, Alice," said Nurse Sue.

The medical barber slipped behind me and took off the wheelchair brake. The jolt of the brake being removed made my heart jump.

This is really happening. I am really having my head shaved.

Both my hands grabbed my stomach to keep it from flipping. It flipped anyway. As the medical barber wheeled me by the girl in the wheelchair, she smiled.

"Want to come watch?" I asked.

I don't know why I said it. Maybe I was scared to be alone and she looked alone, and together, at least we'd be . . . together.

"Yeah!" she said, smiling so I could see every single round, white tooth in her mouth.

"What's going on, Alice?" asked a voice from the room we were sitting outside.

"A girl is going to have her head shaved!" Alice yelled.

"I want to see too!" said the voice.

Someone else called from the room across the hall. "Me too!"

"See what?" Another voice called out from somewhere. A bunch of heads peeked out from different doorways, making me feel as if I were in that scene from the movie *The Wizard of Oz* when Glinda, the Good Witch of the South, told the munchkins they could come out after Dorothy's house killed the Wicked Witch of the East.

The medical barber and I looked back at Nurse Sue behind the desk, and she frowned at us. "She said it, not me," he said.

"Pleeease!" a voice came from yet another room.

Nurse Sue took a deep breath in through her nose. "Okay," she said. And the hallway burst out in cheers. "Go set up Marsha while I get these guys in there."

"Masha," said Alice. "Her name is Masha."

I looked back at Alice in surprise as my medical barber wheeled me away. And she winked.

*   *   *

When Nurse Sue got all the kids in the rec room there were enough bubble bags on sticks to fill about three complete aisles at Wal-Mart, if Wal-Mart sold bubble bags on sticks, which it probably does because it sells everything else. It also sounded like we were in an aisle at Wal-Mart. For a bunch of sick kids, they were pretty noisy. No one would stop talking even though Nurse Sue said, "Excuse me," like, ten times.

Finally, the medical barber put a finger and his thumb in his mouth and gave a loud whistle.

"Attention, everyone! Nurse Sue will take you right back to your rooms if you don't behave. This may not be surgery, but I need to be able to think," he shouted.

The threat of missing the event shut them up. Everyone settled into their wheelchairs, or onto the floor, or on top of the little tables stacked with coloring books.

My medical barber waited until the room was completely silent, and then he removed Mrs. Song's hat.

There were gasps and squeals. I could feel my lips wiggling to keep from frowning and my cheeks being pulled toward the tile floor. There were about twenty-five pairs of eyes, and they were all staring at me.

I looked over at Alice, and she gave me a thumbs-up.

"I'd like everyone to meet Marsha," announced Nurse Sue.

Alice and I locked eyes again, and Alice rolled hers in response to Nurse Sue messing up my name for the millionth time. Her eye roll made a happy spark shoot through my chest. I was Masha Sweet, and I wasn't the only one who knew it.

"As you can see, she has a few flowers glued into her hair, and we're going to get them out," announced Nurse Sue.

"Can I touch one first?" a kid's voice called out from the crowd.

"Sure," I whispered.

A small girl with a bandage over one eye like a pirate reached out her tiny fingers and touched a flower on my head. Her touch lit another happy spark. This one tingled right up my spine.

Now everybody wanted to touch my head. A couple of them gave a tug or two (or three) at the daisies and laughed out loud when they didn't budge. They started asking me questions: Did it hurt? Why was my hair green? Were daisies my favorite flower? Could they have one of them when it was over? What happened to my arm? What happened to my eye? (I ignored those last two.) They smiled and chatted at me and laughed. Who knew that your head becoming a dinner-table centerpiece could actually make you fit in!

Everyone took their seats or wheelchairs.

The nurse wrapped a sheet around my shoulders. My medical barber smeared some gel or cream onto my scalp. It felt cold, but it didn't burn or anything.

"The gel will help loosen the glue from your head. We can't detach it from your actual hair, but the gel will help us get most of it off your scalp," explained my medical barber.

I wasn't totally sure what he meant, but I nodded.

He worked the gel into my scalp. It felt exactly like I was getting my hair washed and cut at the Clip 'n' Snip where Sunny and I always got our hair cut, except instead of a mirror there was a group of kids in front of me. Then there was the sound of the electric razor.

The "*zzzzz*" made the hairs on my skin stand up, and I could actually feel the dust in the air landing on my one bare arm. My fingers squeezed the wheelchair to keep my body in a sitting position. Even my neck

126

muscles seemed to react to the buzz of the razor, and they had trouble holding my head up straight, letting it wobble to the left and right.

A small voice called out from the crowd, "Don't worry, it will be over soon."

Tears filled my eyes, but I opened them wide and willed them to stay right where they were, sitting on my lashes. I was going to look brave even if I wasn't actually brave. I mean, they had all obviously gone through a ton more than I was about to. But even with that thought glued to my head along with the flowers, my breath still seemed to get stuck halfway down my throat. *Sunny Sweet is going to be sorry! Sunny Sweet is going to be sorry! Sunny Sweet is going to be sorry!* I repeated it inside my head over and over and over again, even though, weirdly, I didn't feel so mad anymore. I was just clinging to the saying of it, hoping that at least pretending to be mad would make me feel better.

The razor touched down on my scalp and then made its way across again and again like a lawn mower neatly cutting grass—minus the nice, sweet smell of freshly cut grass, of course. I never let go of the arms of the wheelchair, and I never moved. I stared out at the gray-and-green tiles on the floor of the rec room, while my head became lighter and lighter. You can't believe how heavy hair is until you don't have it anymore.

Out of the corner of my eye I could see light-green

128

clumps of my hair mixed with daisies falling past. I sat still as a stone in the chair. I was too scared that if I moved, I'd lose it. After that one small voice, there were no others. Everyone seemed to be holding their breath along with me.

Then it was done.

The room stayed silent. The medical barber handed me a mirror. I looked into it. And then I looked up because I couldn't look into it anymore.

And in that moment I forgot all about being brave. I couldn't imagine a good thing ever happening in the world again. It felt as if ice cream, kittens, and roller coasters had all been wiped off the face of the earth in one big, horrible wave.

Then Alice started clapping. And then they all started clapping. The sound of their applause snapped the ice-cream-less world right in two, and my chest flooded with a happy warmness . . . which overflowed right out of my eyes. But because I had held my tears in so long, they didn't roll down my cheeks like they should have. They burst from my eyes and landed on my lap.

"She needs her mommy," said that same little voice that had asked to touch a flower.

"We called her mommy, Simone," answered Nurse Sue. "But she isn't home, and Marsha can't remember her mommy's phone number at work."

"Why don't you call her school? They'll probably have it," said a boy's voice.

I wiped the tears out of my eyes with the palm of my hand and looked at the kid with the big idea. He was a boy sitting on one of the little tables with his head wrapped in a hard white shell. But even with an egg on his head, I could tell that he was cute.

All of a sudden my own head felt really, really cold.

Not Blending

I was allowed out of the wheelchair now that I wasn't a real patient anymore, and I helped Nurse Sue get everyone back to their rooms while the medical barber cleaned up the mess that had been attached to my head for the last few hours. I liked helping the nurse. Plus it kept me from racing down to the bathroom and staring at myself in the mirror.

You had to be really careful with the rolling bubble sticks, which I found out were filled with medicine, not water, and it wasn't easy to steer wheelchairs and get broken legs through doorways without rebreaking them, especially with one arm in a cast! Probably if my arm were really broken, I wouldn't have been able to do it. Luckily, no one noticed that I was able to make pretty good use of a "bad" arm.

I made sure to wheel Alice back last. I wanted to say thanks, but I didn't exactly know what to thank her for, so all I did was take off her brake the way Nurse Sue showed me, wheel her out of the rec room, and ask, "Which way?" when we got out to the hall.

"Right," she said. "And it's the third door on the right."

When I got her into her room, I wheeled her into the corner by the window and turned her in a circle so she was facing the door.

Her side of the room was kind of messy, with textbooks and crumpled paper mixed up with headphones and chip wrappers and stepped-on blankets. The mess was moving in a bigish mass over to the other side of the room, where it looked like the bed was empty and there was no patient. The window was covered in greeting cards, all taped up at an angle, and there were a bunch of those silvery balloons hovering a little too close to the top of the table next to her hospital bed. I wanted to stay, to talk to her, but I couldn't think of anything to say, so I just said, "See ya, Alice."

"See ya, Masha," she said.

I turned to smile at her.

"Masha," she said. "How did you get to the hospital if your mom didn't bring you?"

"That's a good question," I told her.

"Sit," she said.

I looked around and chose the empty bed, just so I didn't disturb all the stuff teetering in a tall pile on the chair next to her bed.

"I came with my neighbor, Mrs. Song. She had an accident this morning on her bike."

"What kind of accident?" Alice asked.

"She crashed into our garbage cans. I don't even know why she was riding a bike. I'd never seen her ride one before."

"Maybe that's why she crashed . . . because she didn't know how to ride one," Alice said.

"No, she fainted—at least that's what the guys in the ambulance said."

"You called the ambulance?"

"Yeah, it was my first time calling 911. It was so weird that it actually works, you know?"

"Yeah?" she said. "I've never called 911. So did she die?" she asked.

"Mrs. Song? No! She didn't die. She's fine. She's still down in the ER."

Alice turned in her wheelchair so she was completely facing me. "So when does the part of the story happen where you get those flowers stuck in your green hair, you get a black eye, and you break your arm?" she asked.

Alice's eyes were so dark that they seemed to be looking at me harder than normal eyes, as if I were a test that she was determined to do well on. And her mouth fell into an extracurvy smile. She was waiting for my story, and I wanted to tell it. Not only did I want to tell her the story of what happened today, but I wanted to tell her the whole story.

"That story starts back in Pennsylvania."

"I'm not going anywhere soon," she said, nodding her head at her messy side of the room. And then she folded her hands together and put them under her chin, signaling to me that she was ready.

I told her about living in Pennsylvania and my old house. I told her about how my dad was the principal of my school and how I used to get to go in on Saturdays and play in the gym with all the millions of basketballs and volleyballs from the gym closet. I told her about how my mom had announced that she and my dad were getting a divorce and that we were moving to New Jersey, where she had grown up. Then I told her about Nicole and Alex and being the new kid at school and how I didn't have that many good friends. And finally I told her about how Sunny had gotten up in the middle of the night, crept into my room, and glued plastic flowers on to my head while I was sleeping so the girls at school would notice me.

Alice gave a scream at that part. It made my heart jump, but not in an "I am stupid" kind of way, in a "how cool to make people scream by just telling them a story" kind of way. It made us both break down laughing, which sounded more like snorting because we were both laughing so hard.

"Did you and your sister get into a fistfight and she punched you in the eye and broke your arm?" Alice squealed.

It was my turn to scream. "No! Sunny didn't do the other stuff. I did that to myself."

And then I told Alice the rest of the story ... about the freezer and the peanut butter, about the cast and the mean nurse, and about Sunny taking me to the basement. And just because Alice loved the stories, I got into telling a few more about Sunny. I told her about poor Eddie the gerbil, and then I told her

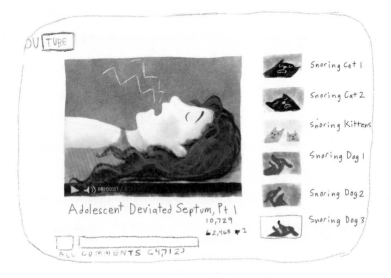

OU TUBE

Adolescent Deviated Septum, Pt 1
00:00:01 /
10,729
62,463 🖒 1

Snoring Cat 1

Snoring Cat 2

Snoring Kittens

Snoring Dog 1

Snoring Dog 2

Snoring Dog 3

ALL COMMENTS (47,127)

about the time that Sunny put a video of me snoring on YouTube. "She said she was doing a study on adolescent deviated septums. You know, when there's something wrong inside your nose. It turned out that nothing was wrong with my nose and that I just snored. It got, like, ten thousand hits."

"She did not do that!" Alice yelled.

"She did."

I loved it that Alice was laughing. For the first time, it made me laugh at the stuff that Sunny did.

"My older brother is awful too," Alice said. "Not because he's the devil, but because he's an angel. He never does *anything* wrong. He's so good all the time so I can be the bad one if I want."

"Wow, that's the strangest thing I ever heard. So you can be bad?"

"Yeah, because of this," she said, motioning to the wheelchair. "But it's no fun to be bad when someone's letting you. My brother lets me. My parents let me. They let me get my ear pierced up here," she said, pointing to a diamond stud in the top of her ear that I hadn't really noticed before. "They let me get a D in math. And when I stole a hat from a store last winter they just paid for it. They never even yelled or told me not to do it again or anything."

"You got a D in math." I gasped.

Alice laughed. "You're so funny, Masha. Most kids I know would think the hat was worse, not the bad grade. And just so you know, I got an F in gym too."

"Really?"

"No, Masha, not really! I can't play gym." She giggled.

"Oh yeah," I said. And then I stopped and looked at her. She instantly knew my thoughts.

"What?" she asked.

"Are you . . . dying, Alice?" I asked her.

"No, Marsha, I'm not dying. Are you dying?" Alice shot back.

"Uh," I said.

Alice laughed. "We're all dying, Masha! One day."

I thought about it a second, and she was right. "Hey, Alice, do you think your hair keeps growing after you die, you know, like your fingernails?"

138

"You're sick." Alice giggled.

We started laughing again, and I kicked the stack of junk on the chair by accident and the whole mess slid to the floor, which just made us laugh harder.

"I wish you could stay here," Alice said. And then she blurted, "I like it that you complain, and freak out, and knock stuff over, and talk about stuff like dying. I think it's so cool."

"Really?" I asked. "Because I can complain and freak out all the time if you want."

We laughed.

"So do you know the kid with the egg on his head?" I asked.

"Michael Capezzi," she said.

"I think he's cute."

"Me too," she answered. Then she added, "I know that you're really mad at your sister right now, but I'm kind of glad that she glued flowers to your head, because I got to meet you." Her dark eyes looked down at the mess on her floor, and her eyelashes made feathery shadows run down her cheeks.

"Marsha!" Nurse Sue called from the hall.

Alice and I looked at each other and then fell apart laughing.

"Coming," I managed to shout back.

*   *   *

140

By the time I got to the front desk, Nurse Sue had already called my school and was dialing my mother's work number.

"Finally, Marsha," she said, "we'll be able to get you your mother."

"But I don't want to go home," I whispered as I ran my hand across the top of my empty head. She hadn't heard me—not that I had actually meant her to—and I just watched her finish dialing the telephone and then listened to the quiet ring coming from under her ear.

I heard the second ring.

My mother always takes forever to pick up her phone. It's as if she doesn't really hear it until the third ring.

There was a loud beeping from a panel on the desk in front of Nurse Sue that seemed to display all of the room numbers on it, and a light lit up room number 216. Nurse Sue looked down the hallway and then she hopped up and handed me the phone.

"I'll be right back," she said, taking off toward room 216.

141

I heard the third ring and knew my mother would pick up in the next second. But that was all the time I needed to form my plan. I couldn't believe what I was about to do. Being nearly bald had somehow also made me want to be brave.

"Jane Sweet."

"Hi, Mom."

"Hi, Masha sweetie, how's it going? How do you feel?"

My eyes started watering, and I had the most awful urge to sniff. But I didn't want her to know I was crying, so I just wiped my nose with the back of my wrist and told her I felt fine. What I really wanted to tell her was everything . . . about Mrs. Song, and Calvin's disease, and my cast, and meeting Alice, and how I was nearly bald, and, weirdly, even about that cute kid with the egg head. But most of all I wanted to tell her how I knew I hadn't been acting the nicest toward Sunny and that I loved her, and that I wasn't mad about the move anymore. But I didn't.

"What time are you going to be home?" I said, trying to sound normal, but instead my words came out faint and filled with air. My mom didn't seem to notice.

"I'm going to pick up Sunny after school in about a half hour and then I'll be home," she said.

I forgot about Sunny and school! "No, no, Mom, I'll get her. I can walk right over."

"But your hair, Masha," she said.

"I'll wear a hat. No problem," I told her.

She was quiet for a moment. Then she said softly, "Hey, a few of the people in the office gave me some good ideas about how to get the plastic flowers off."

"Really?" I gulped. "Cool, Mom. Okay, I'll see you after work." I had to push the words from deep inside my chest. I could tell by the way she said good-bye and hung up that I had made her happy. I knew that she'd be upset when she saw my head . . . and everything else, but since I didn't have Calvin's disease, the cast was already dried on my arm, my hair would grow back, my eye would heal, and there was a bus outside that would take us close to home, I knew that I could leave her to finish her day and tell her all about it later (or at least, *mostly* all about it, leaving out the parts that might get me in trouble). If I could get my head shaved, I could get my little sister and me home on the bus alone.

Even as I was having these brave thoughts about standing up out of this chair and walking out of the hospital, my heart wasn't totally convinced. In fact, it was kind of bobbing about in my chest, feeling a little alone.

I looked up and down the halls, but they were empty except for some carts filled with blankets and towels and stuff. I could hear activity going on inside the rooms, but none of it had anything to do with me. Nurse Sue was nowhere in sight.

I ran my hand over the top of my bald head, and then in some kind of panic reflex, like someone had just hit my knee with a tiny hammer, I picked up the phone to call my mother back. My fingers hovered over the buttons. Argh! I didn't know the number! Without my dumb cell phone, I didn't know *anybody's* telephone number.

Except I did.

I knew Sunny's.

I dialed those ten digits. The phone rang.

"Hello," she said.

"Uh, hi, Sunny, it's me."

"Masha, you're calling me!" she shouted into the phone, making my heart ache. "Where are you? Are you still up in pediatrics?"

"Yes. Listen," I told her, "I think we should bust out of here."

"Really?" she breathed. "When?"

"I think . . . now," I told her, looking around the hospital corridor and having the feeling of no longer belonging here.

"I'll meet you out front," she said, out of breath from excitement. "And Masha," she added, "I promise I'm going to get those flowers off your head. And I'm going to fix your hair too, okay?"

"Okay," I said, rubbing my hand over my baldness.

She hung up.

We were going home.

Two minutes later, Nurse Sue came hurrying back down the hall.

"My mom said she'll be here as soon as she can," I told her.

But Nurse Sue didn't hear me. Instead, she picked up the phone I had just set down and dialed.

"Security?" she asked. "I need to report a missing patient. Yes. Pediatrics. Yes, Michael Capezzi. Yes, I'll hold."

Hey, the boy with the egg on his head just stole my idea!

Sunny Sweet Is
So Sorry

Nurse Sue?"

"Yes," she said, still staring at the spot on her desk
that she had been staring at since security asked her to
hold—I guess she didn't want to risk not being in the
same position when they came back to the phone. A
clump of her dark hair was out of her bun and hanging down over her ear, and she chewed on her lip as
she waited. She looked younger than I first thought.

"I'm all itchy from getting my hair cut," I told her.
"I'm going to go to the bathroom and clean up. I may
be in there for a little while."

She took a quick breath in and looked up at me, and I was sure that she absolutely knew my entire plan.

"Sure, honey," she said. "Down the hall and on your right-hand side, you'll find a linen closet with towels and washcloths and scrubs. The bathroom will be across the hall from the closet." She pointed and gave me a tight smile, and then she went back to staring at her desk.

"Thanks," I said, taking a quiet, deep breath and getting up.

Another nurse came rushing to the desk. I was sure that this nurse was completely on to me. I stopped and stood by my chair, waiting to be caught.

"Sue?" she said, not even noticing me standing there.

"I know," Nurse Sue said. "Again! I don't know why he does this."

They seemed distracted, and I used the moment to sneak back down the hall to Alice's room.

"I came to say good-bye," I said.

Alice didn't say anything. She just looked at me

148

with those round, dark eyes. I could tell that she was struggling to keep her mouth in the shape of her curvy smile.

My eyes scanned the messy hospital room for her cell phone, and I spotted it lying almost under the bed. I got down on my knees, grabbed it, handed it to her, and told her my cell phone number.

Her smile was real. "I'll call you later," she said. And then she peeked behind me. "Is your mom here?"

"Uh, no," I told her. I guess I must have looked sneaky, because she dipped her head toward me and asked, "How are you getting home, Masha?"

"Getting home, hmm," I said.

"What is it?" Alice asked.

"Well, I'm breaking out. I'm meeting my little sister out front, and we're taking the bus home."

I must have looked just like I felt, because she said, "You can do it, Masha."

"I can." I smiled. "And if I make it home on the bus, then I can make it back on the bus. How about I come visit you after school tomorrow?" The thought of school sent a whirl of fear flying around my stomach. My hand went up to my head and rubbed the place where my hair had been. "If I survive school, that is."

"You'll survive," Alice said.

And I knew that I would survive, because now I had someone who was going to listen to every horrible detail of how hard it was.

I nodded my head. And then I bent down and hugged her ponytailed head, clunking my giant cast into her shoulder blade. She smelled like a warm sweatshirt that had just come out of the dryer.

I walked to the door and turned around to say good-bye one more time. I knew that I didn't have to tell her not to say anything about my leaving on my own; she just wouldn't.

"See you tomorrow," I told her.

Alice gave me the "rock on" sign. And I turned

and left. As I started down the hall, it felt like my heart was smiling.

*   *   *

I walked to the linen closet and pulled out a wash-cloth and towel and also a pair of plain blue hospital pants and a blue hospital shirt, and then went into the bathroom. It was one thing to run around with ele-phants all over you in a hospital, but I wasn't going to take the bus home dressed like this. After I changed, I stood and stared at myself in the mirror. When I was down in the basement peering into that paper-towel dispenser, I really thought for sure that I couldn't possibly look worse than I did right then. I was wrong.

I closed my eyes so I could unglue myself from the mirror, and then I walked out of the bathroom with-out looking back.

I walked straight out of pediatrics and wandered up and down a few random hallways looking for an intersection with some signs telling me where I was and which way to go. The first sign I found was one pointing out the direction of the emergency room. I stopped and whispered a good-bye to Mrs. Song. One more hallway and I saw it, MAIN LOBBY with a comforting arrow.

I wondered if Thelma, the lollipop lady, would remember me, but before I reached the lobby, I turned a corner and there was Sunny, standing down the hall, still wearing her white lab coat.

She froze, staring at me with her big, spooky eyes. I walked slowly toward her, watching those eyes get bigger and bigger with every step I took. When I finally got about ten steps away, she screamed and fell onto her knobby little knees right there in the hallway. I guess I did look pretty scary, but strangely, I also felt a little bit cool. Maybe I would ask my mom if I could get a diamond stud in the top of my ear like Alice's. I bet it would really stand out with my bald head and black eye.

When Sunny got done screaming, she held her cheeks in her hands, and her face looked like the sad mask that my English teacher, Ms. Lee, had hanging in her classroom. I think it's the tragedy one. "Like it?" I asked. "You did it."

152

But even before I was done saying it, I wished that I could suck it back in. I wanted to be a better me . . . a me that liked her little sister, even if she was the devil.

And then Sunny did the weirdest thing. She started to cry, hard . . . like a real six-year-old and not like an evil genius six-year-old.

Sunny Sweet was finally sorry.

And now I didn't want her to be!

"Oh, Sunny," I said, running over to her. "It's okay, it's okay." I knelt down on the floor and wrapped my good arm around her little shoulders and whispered into her ear, "I kind of like it."

"Really?" she asked, looking up at me with the truest glow of love you ever saw.

And in that moment, I realized that yes, I *really* did.

"Girls," came a voice . . . a mean voice.

Sunny and I stared down the hallway. There, with his hands on his hips, stood the mean nurse!

Run!

Never in my life have I ever run from trouble. And I probably wouldn't have run if it weren't for Sunny, who whispered, "We need to separate. I'll meet you at the bus stop," and then spit, "Run!" directly into my face.

She took off, and I took off right after her. When we got to the end of the hall, she hooked right and I flew left.

I snapped my head around for one last look behind me at the same time Sunny turned to look back at me. She smiled that evil little smile of hers, and for the first time in my life, it sent a huge smile shooting across my own face. And then I spun around and ran.

I made the first turn I could and jetted up a set of stairs and out into another hallway. I had no idea where I was, but I didn't stop to find out. I hurried past a nurses' station, struggling to catch my breath and look like I hadn't just robbed a bank or something. When I got around the corner, I decided to pull my cast inside my shirt. That way, if the mean nurse asked if anyone had seen a kid with an orange cast, they would have to say no.

I came upon a group of elevators and hit both the up and down buttons. I was going to take the first one that opened. The light pinged. I was going down.

When the door opened, I poked my head out. I was on the first floor, but I didn't know where. I stepped out and headed in the only direction that I could: left.

I walked past office after office. There were people in them, but no one looked up from their computers as I walked by. When I passed by a dark office, I noticed a guy dumping garbage from a can into a big bin—a custodian.

"Hi," I said. "I'm a little lost. I was supposed to meet my mom in front of the hospital and I took a wrong turn." I tried to pull my cast under my shirt as close to my body as possible so he wouldn't notice. But I also knew that in this place, no matter what you looked like, people treated you as if you were normal. I swear I could be carrying a basket of slithering snakes and no one would even blink!

"You did take a wrong turn," he said, not looking at my arm at all. "If you go down this hallway and take a right, all you have to do is follow the signs that say main lobby. It's a bit of a walk."

"Is that the Shapiro main lobby?" I asked.

"Yes, it is." He smiled.

"Thanks," I said, giving him a salute, although I'm not sure why. He saluted back. And I took off.

I followed his directions, my heart pounding with every bend in the hallway. The closer I got to the Shapiro main lobby, the harder it was to breathe. Spotting a bathroom, I dodged inside and closed the door, locking it behind me. I leaned against the wall and closed my eyes, willing my heart to chill out. I knew I had to keep going. Sunny would be waiting. But it felt so good to be safe. I glanced in the mirror but then looked away. I focused on the WASH YOUR HANDS sign and wondered where Sunny was. Maybe she was already out at the bus stop. I looked over at the door. I had to go back out there. I looked back in the mirror. There was no way to disguise myself. I was bald, with a black eye and one arm. The only option was to open that door and get out of the hospital as fast as I could. I stepped out and started down the hall at a gallop.

After what felt like seventeen million hospital hallways, I found myself creeping into the Shapiro main lobby. My knees were actually knocking together. I was so close. I told myself that if I saw the mean nurse, I could just make a run for it, but I wasn't sure that I'd be brave enough to run again. It was one thing with Sunny and me doing it together, but it was another thing doing it alone.

I tiptoed into the lobby. I was now officially in

no-man's-land—out of the hall but not out of the door. There were two ladies sitting on the couches that Sunny had been climbing around on earlier, and an unfamiliar lady was at Thelma's desk. The doors were about twenty steps away. I wanted to run so badly, but I knew that I would just attract attention if I did. I forced myself to walk slowly, counting my steps in my head as I went. "One, two, three, four, five . . ."

I was dying to look around and see if the mean nurse was near, but I didn't; I kept my attention on the glass doors.

"Six, seven, eight, nine, ten."

The phone at the desk rang, and my legs just about collapsed underneath me.

"Eleven, twelve, thirteen, fourteen-fifteen-six-seven-eight-nine-twenty!" And I was out. I pulled my cast out of my shirt and ran down the front walk. The bus stop was right where Sunny said it would be. I looked up and down the street, but she wasn't there. It felt like someone kicked me right in my heart. *Maybe he caught her?*

I stopped on the sidewalk and tried to decide what to do. Should I go back in? I turned to face the

hospital's front doors. Could I do this? Could I walk back in there? I had to find her. My heart pounded in my temples as I took my first slow steps back to the front doors. I had to get Sunny. I started to run.

"Masha!"

I turned around with the biggest smile ever. There was Sunny Sweet, standing behind a giant stone flowerpot by the bus stop. But the smile quickly fell from my face.

"Sunny," I whispered, "no!"

I ran toward her. "No, no, no!"

She stood as still as the stone flowerpot next to her . . . and she was bald!

"Sunny, why?" I asked, dropping to my knees in front of her.

She rubbed her bare little head and shrugged.

I threw my arms around her and hugged her tight.

Sisters

How did you do it?" I asked.

We sat on the bench by the bus stop. According to Sunny's bus app, our bus was number 68, and we needed to get off at Washington Street and Elm Avenue. The bus was due to arrive in three minutes, although it was nowhere in sight. An afternoon breeze swished through the pansies in the big stone pots. I shivered. It was actually a little chilly not having hair.

"After I left you," Sunny said, "I ran back down to the lab. I had seen the depilatory creams in the cabinet when I was searching for the ingredients to dissolve the glue on your head. They use them for surgery patients."

"What's a depilatory?"

"It's usually calcium thioglycolate or potassium thioglycolate. They are chemicals that weaken the hair so it falls right out. It took three minutes."

"Why didn't they use that stuff on me?" I asked.

"You wouldn't want to have mixed the chemicals from the depilatory cream with the chemicals I used to create the glue. It would have changed the chemicals."

"And what is so bad about that?"

"Have you ever seen a firework explode?" she asked.

"Yes."

"That is an example of a chemical change," she said. "It was better that they just shaved you."

I laughed. "You're so weird, Sunny, but I'm glad you're my sister."

She giggled back at me and threw her little bald head in my lap.

People began to collect around us at the bus stop,

and I saw their eyes land on Sunny and me for a second before they quickly looked away. I thought about Mrs. Song's hat. I had left it up in pediatrics, but I didn't need it anymore. A bald head or a big hat, what did it matter? I didn't blend in, and I was okay with that.

Finally the large, round headlights of the bus caught my eye.

"Come on, Sunny."

We walked to the curb, straining to see what number it was. It was number 68, our bus. We were as good as home.

The bus's breaks squealed and then hissed as it came to a stop. The doors swung open with a screech. This was when it occurred to me . . . we didn't have any money.

Sunny moved to get in line for the bus. I held her back, moving us out of the line. "We don't have money," I whispered.

She frowned. "Maybe if we tell the driver we're only going a few stops he'll let us on?"

"Maybe," I croaked, even though I didn't believe it.

The small crowd of people was slowly making its way onto the bus. I looked down at Sunny and then back at the hospital. I couldn't stop myself from hopping up and down and doing a couple of silly twirls with my arms flapping about. We had to get on that bus but I didn't know how, and it was like my arms and legs were itching to grab Sunny and leap in.

"Come on," said a voice from behind me.

I turned. It was Michael Capezzi!

He moved toward the back of the bus where the doors were opened to let people off and motioned for me and Sunny to follow. As the last person stepped off the bus, he climbed on. I grabbed Sunny's elbow and we followed.

He snaked around the pole and plopped into a seat. I pulled Sunny down into the two seats opposite him. My eyes darted around at the people sitting near us. Had any of them noticed? Would they say something? I was panting and sweating like I'd just run ten miles.

"So, you guys are breaking out of the hospital too, huh?" Michael didn't seem to be scared or nervous about sneaking onto the bus.

"*Technically* it's not breaking out because we weren't locked in," Sunny said.

"Thanks for . . . helping us," I said. "How did you know that we needed to get on the bus?"

"You looked like you needed to get on." He laughed. "Nice heads, by the way," he added, smiling.

I searched for something cool to say back but couldn't think of anything except, "Same to you."

He smiled again. "You're funny."

I liked his smile. His mouth was large and seemed to sit on his face in a wide, twitchy kind of way, like he was holding that smile back from breaking out all over his face. His eyes were a light brown with really black lashes. His stare made me feel a weird pressure in my chest, making it hard to take anything but tiny breaths that I knew wouldn't keep me alive for long. But even the thought of not breathing didn't stop me from being really happy that Michael had appeared out of nowhere and saved us.

"So where are you guys going?" he asked.

"We're going home," Sunny said. I was glad she answered because I definitely couldn't breathe and talk at the same time. "What's wrong with your head?" she asked.

"Sunny," I hissed.

"No, that's okay." He shrugged. "I have a tumor. Oh wait," he added, "*technically* I had a tumor. It's gone now."

He and I laughed. Sunny didn't. She didn't get it. She just started in on tumors. She actually loved tumors. "Brain Tumor Week" on the Discovery Fit & Health channel was like Sunny's "Shark Week." She'd sit in front of the television for hours while some guy with the most boring voice ever droned on and on in Latin or something.

Michael listened to Sunny blab about tumors, but he kept looking at me out of the corner of his eye. I sat with the rumble of the motor of the bus underneath me and snuck looks back at him. I couldn't tell if it was the heat of the motor or those eyes looking over at me, but little drops of sweat were trickling down the back of my hospital shirt. How could someone noticing you make you hot and itchy *and* happy? But it did.

"Why did you break out of the hospital?" I asked, without having made any plans at all on opening my

168

mouth. I had interrupted Sunny, but she didn't notice. She was too busy googling stuff about brain tumors on her phone.

He looked up and down at my bald head and hospital clothes and asked, "Why did you break out of the hospital?"

We both laughed, and he used the moment to move over to the seats in front of ours, which made the saliva in my mouth instantly dry up.

"I'm Michael," he said, putting out his hand over the top of the seat back. His eyes were so close that I almost couldn't see them.

"I'm Masha," I said, shaking his hand awkwardly. "And this is my little sister, Sunny."

"Hi, Masha. Hi, Sunny."

He got my name right. This was the second time today that someone got my name right.

Sunny looked up from her phone. "You know what Caroline Alvinia told me?"

Michael and I looked at each other and then back at Sunny, and shrugged.

"She said that every time a boy talks to your older sister, you are supposed to get down on the ground and bite his ankles."

"Why?" he and I said together.

"I don't know, I'm just repeating what she told me," said Sunny. "I thought maybe you guys would know."

"Washington Street and Elm Avenue," said the computer-generated woman's voice that called out all the stops.

"We gotta go," I said, jumping up and starting for the door.

"Bye, Masha," he said. "Hey—and Sunny, you can bite my ankles next time, okay?"

"Okay," Sunny said.

Next time. I don't know why it felt as if someone were tickling the inside of my chest with a feather when he said that, but it did.

"Bye," I whispered, looking back at him but only seeing him as a blob in the seat because of the whole feather thing.

I couldn't get the goofy smile off my face for the

entire eight-block walk home. It was still there when I caught sight of my mother pulling into our driveway. I guess Mom had decided to come home early, even though I had told her not to.

Sunny and I crossed the street, stepping over the garbage by the curb. I spotted my cell phone lying in the gutter and picked it up. My mom climbed out of her car.

When her eyes caught sight of Sunny and me, her jaw dropped. That's a saying—your jaw dropping—but it's a saying because it really happens; your jaw really can drop.

Sunny ran to her and hugged her around her waist. I couldn't hold back, so I ran over too, hugging her right over the top of Sunny. My mom smelled like clean

carpets mixed with a hint of dry-erase marker. It smelled so good. "We're fine, Mom. We really are."

I stood back from her, and Sunny joined me, holding on to my hand. I looked right into my mother's eyes and smiled. "We're fine."

"Okay, Masha," she said. "Okay." And her tone made me feel like she totally believed me and that everything was okay.

My cell phone rang.

My mom jumped and then looked down at me in surprise. My phone was ringing and it obviously wasn't Sunny calling.

"Oh," I said. "Guess what happened today?"

My mother stared at me.

"I made a friend," I said. "Her name is Alice."

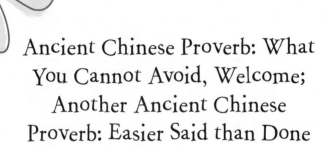

Ancient Chinese Proverb: What You Cannot Avoid, Welcome; Another Ancient Chinese Proverb: Easier Said than Done

Let me walk you into school," my mom said.

"No, Mom, please. I can do it," I repeated for the tenth time. This was going to be hard enough without my mother watching.

"Okay." She sighed.

My mom felt so guilty over my head being shaved that she agreed to let me keep the cast. I had explained that it would be easier for me to go back to school bald if I could do it with my orange cast on. She even called the hospital, getting me completely off the hook. And then she called school and told them that I'd had a little "bike accident." All this had made me pretty happy as I got into bed last night, but it wasn't helping me this morning. The three of us sat in the parking lot watching streams of buses and cars and people and kids all heading toward the school . . . all heading toward *my bald head*. I knew I couldn't hide forever, but I also couldn't bring myself to give up trying just yet.

We waited until almost everyone was in the building, and then Sunny and I finally got out of the car. I gave my mom a big smile to assure her I was okay. Her face glowed with worry through the windshield.

"You know that they don't have to shave your head to test you for a concussion," Sunny said.

"Yes, Sunny, I know. You already said that three times at breakfast. Mom just told the school that because it was easier than explaining your flowers."

"But what about *my* bald head?"

"That's why she also told them that you wanted to be just like your big sister and get a test on your head too, remember?"

"But that makes it sound like I think that you need

174

to have your head shaved for a test that you *don't* need your head shaved for," she whined.

"What?" I asked.

Sunny went on about cat or dog scans or something, but I had stopped listening. My feet slowed with each step, scraping lightly against the sidewalk, until they finally stopped altogether.

Sunny stopped too. "*Zhu ni hao yun*," she said. "It means 'good luck' in Chinese."

"I know what it means," I snapped. But I didn't.

"Hey, Masha," she said, tugging at my arm. "I think it's cool that you're learning Mandarin Chinese. Listen, maybe I should learn Cantonese. Cantonese is the language spoken in southern China and Hong Kong. That way, when we go to China one day, you can speak Mandarin and I can speak Cantonese, and we'll be able to talk to everyone!"

I wanted to be mad at her. But when I looked down at her little bald head, I just couldn't. "There are more than 1.3 billion people living in China," I said, quoting from page three of my *Longman Active Study English-Chinese Dictionary*. "That's a whole lot of talking!"

Sunny giggled. I took her hand, and together we started toward the front doors of school. There were more than 1.3 billion things I'd rather be doing right now other than walking into my school bald, but as far as I could see, there wasn't one single way out of it.

The warm, stuffy air inside the building hit me in the face. I said a quick good-bye to my little sister and then, with a hurricane swirling in my stomach, I tiptoed through the deserted hallways until I reached my homeroom.

The door was open. I hovered across the hall, clutching my absentee note from my mother. A huge urge to run swept over me, and my legs wobbled with the effort not to do it. I reminded myself how soon I'd be with Alice, telling her all about this horrible moment. And then, with nothing left to stop me, I sucked in my breath as hard as I could and walked through the door.

I can't remember who saw me first. I just remember the moment when they *all* saw me. There was silence. And then there were wide-open eyes. And then gasps. And finally, after about five *very long seconds*, there came a burst of laughter. Mostly everything was a blur, although not the sight of Alex and Nicole looking at each other and laughing. That was pretty clear. My homeroom teacher, Mr. Valentino, put a fast end to it. "That's it, everyone. Settle down."

He stopped writing his notes on the whiteboard and hurried over to me. "How're you doing? I heard about your accident." I handed him my note. He took it, along with my good arm, and helped me toward my seat, even though I really didn't need any help. All heads swerved to watch us make our way across the silent classroom.

"As you can see, Masha had a little accident," he announced, his voice echoing across the quiet room. Then he turned directly to me. "We're all so thankful you're okay." He pulled out my chair, and I sat down. Then he made his way back to the front of the classroom, but no one's eyes followed him. They all stayed on me.

My head felt light and empty. It ached from my bad decision not to wear a hat. We aren't allowed to wear hats in school, but my mom said she'd ask if they could make an exception for me. I stupidly said no. Sunny had suggested that she wrap my head in gauze so I'd look a little like Michael Capezzi. Again, I said no. But now I was thinking that sporting the mummy look would have been better than this terrible naked feeling.

The only sound in the room was the soft squeaking of Mr. Valentino's marker. Then someone's chair scraped the floor, moving so he or she could get a better view of me. It sounded like thunder. I stared straight ahead into nothing. The beating of my heart was actually hurting my ears, and the air in the room refused to go down my throat and into my lungs. I clung to the side of my desk and tried not to die of embarrassment, which I was very, very close to doing, when I felt a light tap on my back.

It was so light that I wasn't sure that it happened until it happened again.

I turned my head to look behind me.

"Did it hurt?" asked the second-smartest kid in school.

It's the first time I think I ever heard Junchao Tao speak. Her bravery reminded me that I, too, was now brave, and I spoke back to her . . . in Chinese.

"You yi dian'er," I said, holding up my thumb and pointer finger to show her that I meant "a little."

Her eyes opened in surprise, and she laughed. Her laugh shocked me. It was huge and deep, like a Santa Claus laugh. And Junchao Tao was about the size of my teddy bear.

"Mei li de hei yan jing," she said. I just stared at her. "Nice black eye," she translated.

I gave her a wink . . . Unfortunately I did it with my black eye. "Ouch."

"Ho-ho-ho," she laughed.

Her jolly chuckle broke the silence, and all at once, everybody wanted to know what happened to my hair, my arm, my eye. Did I get to ride in an ambulance? Yes. Was there a lot of blood? No. How long did I get to wear the cast? That one I just shrugged at. My mom hadn't decided yet.

"Mr. Valentino, Mr. Valentino," Nicole called, swinging her arm in the air. "Doesn't Masha get an elevator key?"

"I almost forgot," he said, walking over to his desk and pulling out a key. "The elevator should make your life a little easier for the next couple of weeks." He made his way to my desk and handed me the golden key. It wasn't really golden, but it felt like it was.

"You should head out for reading group now so you don't get pushed around in the hallway. And remember to leave reading a few minutes early so you miss the crowds coming back for math."

I nodded.

"Mr. Valentino, Mr. Valentino," Alex called, swinging her arm in the air. "Doesn't Masha get to pick someone to carry her books?"

"Sure she can," Mr. Valentino said. "Masha?" he asked, waiting for me to choose someone.

Nicole and Alex sat up straight in their chairs and smiled at me. I had a choice to make . . . and I couldn't believe how easy it was.

"I'd like Junchao to help me," I said.

I didn't look over at Nicole or Alex. Instead, I turned to look at Junchao.

"*Xie xie*," she said.

"You're welcome." I smiled.

A Changed Person

"Two more weeks," I begged.

"One," my mother said.

"One and a half?" I suggested.

"One more week and that cast comes off, Masha," my mother said, not taking her eyes from the road.

We were on our way to the New Jersey State Science Fair for Sunny. The state science fair was regional first, so everyone there today would be from northern New Jersey. Junchao would be there, and maybe a couple more kids from my class at school.

You had to be in the fourth through twelfth grade to compete, although they let Sunny in.

"Anyway," my mother continued, "you should count yourself lucky that I let you keep that fake cast on for an entire week already!"

"It's a real cast, Mom."

"You know what I mean," my mother said with her eyebrows raised in warning. She put on her blinker and pulled off the highway.

"I wish I'd broken my arm." Sunny sighed from the back seat.

"And she's the genius?" I asked.

My mother glared at me. "I'm just kidding, Mom." I laughed. And I *was* just kidding. I mean, if this were last week, I wouldn't have been kidding, but it's not. It's this week. And this week, I am a changed person.

I turned around and looked at my little sister in the backseat of the car. She'd been awfully quiet the entire ride to the science fair. She was wearing a rain jacket and a rain hat with a wide brim, and she was bent over something in a bottle, which I assumed

184

was a piece of her science project. I also assumed the rain jacket and hat were part of the experiment too, since it happened to be a beautiful day. When Sunny felt me looking at her, she looked up at me and smiled. I smiled back.

In the end, life as a bald, black-eyed, broken-armed kid had been pretty great. Junchao and I practiced our Chinese in the elevator every day.

I aced Mrs. Hull's makeup science test. And the entire fifth grade signed my cast (including Nicole and Alex, because I didn't want them to feel left out). I was having such a good time. And now I only had one week left. I rested my bright-orange cast in my lap and petted it like a cat. My favorite spot on it was the spiky letters that read "Michael Capezzi."

"Shawna said I had to have it on for six weeks," I tried.

"Masha Sweet," my mother growled.

"She's getting mad at you," Sunny said.

"You better be quiet or you can go to your stupid science fair by yourself," I shot back at her before I could remember that I was a changed person.

"Masha," my mother gasped, "enough. You'll take her to the fair and help her set up her experiment, and get home together on the bus, just like I've asked you to do. Now, show me the bus and lunch money I gave you. Also, I expect a text at the end of the fair and then a second text when you get home. Mrs. Song said she'd cook you guys dinner tonight since this painting class that I'm taking is going to go pretty late."

Mrs. Song was home from the hospital and doing fantastic. She had gotten her medications mixed up and that was why she had fainted. But they did tell her to stay off the bike for a while. I had been stopping by after school to say, *"Ni hao,"* and see how she was feeling.

I pulled the twenty-dollar bill that my mother had given me from my pocket and waved it in the air next to her head. And then I noticed my mother doing that kind of half-sigh thing where she seemed to keep the other half stuck inside her. I guess nobody can just change overnight, although she had signed up for this painting class today. My mom stopped painting when we moved, so being in this class was a good thing. Plus she was letting me take Sunny home on the bus after the fair. This was actually the second time this week she let us ride the bus alone. On Wednesday she had let Sunny and I take it to visit Alice after school. Then she picked us up at the hospital after she got done at work, and the three of us went for pizza.

"Don't worry, Mom," I told her. "Just have fun at your class. Sunny and I will be fine. And I won't forget to text you. *Both times*."

She shot me a smile. "Okay," she said. And I'm pretty sure that I saw the rest of the sigh slide out.

My cell phone rang.

I quickly pulled it out of my pocket, thinking it was Alice. Instead I saw the word "Sunny" light up my screen.

"Hello."

"Hi, Masha," she said.

"Hi, Sunny."

"Did you think it was going to be Alice?" she asked.

"Yes, I did," I told her.

My mother pulled into the parking lot of a gigantic, unfamiliar high school.

"We're here," Sunny said excitedly into my ear. "I'll talk to you later, okay?"

"Yes, you will," I answered.

And we hung up.

188

Sunny Sweet Is So Dead Meat

Sunny and I waved good-bye to Mom as she pulled out of the parking lot. Then we each picked up a box filled with pieces of Sunny's science experiment and headed toward the doors of the school. Each year the science fair was held at a different school, so neither of us had ever been here before. There's always something kind of spooky about a school on a Saturday, and it's twice as spooky when it's a school you don't know.

"Are we early?" I asked my little sister as I looked around the parking lot. There didn't seem to be many cars in the lot. Or even any cars at all.

"I needed to get here first," she said. "So I told Mommy that the science fair started at ten. It actually starts at eleven."

"Really, Sunny?" I groaned. "I already have to waste an entire Saturday doing this with you when I could have been at the hospital hanging out with Alice." My friend had spina bifida, which meant that her spine didn't close the right way before she was born. She sometimes had to be in the hospital for a few weeks at a time so they could watch her spinal cord as she grew.

Sunny's bony little shoulders drooped, making me feel instantly bad for what I'd said.

"Anyway," I told her, bumping her gently with my arm, "maybe we can visit Alice later tonight. They have late visiting hours on Saturday. And hey, I know," I added, "we can bring the trophy you're gonna win today to show her."

Sunny had won the trophy last year at our old school. In fact, Sunny always won the trophy wherever she went. I guess it was hard not giving the award to a scrawny little six-year-old kid with giant blue eyes and a brain that weighed more than the rest of her body put together.

"Okay, Masha," she said, beaming up at me from under the wide brim of her rain hat. The hat was my mother's, so it was way too big for her and it came down right to the top of her eyelashes. The rain jacket she wore was also my mother's, and it scraped at the pavement of the parking lot as we walked. Looking at her in this crazy rain outfit on this beautiful cloudless spring day, it hit me that I had no idea what her science experiment was about. Sunny was always working on a million different "projects," as she called them, and none of them made any sense to me. But her strange outfit was kind of interesting.

"What's your experiment about, anyway?" I asked.

"It's about people who don't follow the rules of society."

"About what?"

Sunny stopped walking. "It's an experiment about being different," she said slowly. "Like, for example, at school . . . you know how some kids fit in and some kids don't?"

"Um, yeah," I said, surprised that I really did know. "So you're wearing a rain hat and raincoat on a beautiful sunshiny day because you're being different?" I asked.

"Good question," she said, putting down her box in the middle of the parking lot.

I shook my head thoughtfully as if I were completely used to asking good questions. I had lived on this earth for almost double the amount of years that my little sister had, but most days I felt like I'd only managed to develop half of the brain power.

"We have to do something before we go in. It's part of my experiment." Sunny knelt down and started digging in her box. She found what she was searching for and pulled it out. "Here!" she said, jumping to her feet and handing it to me.

"Okay," I said. "It's a bottle of Heinz ketchup."

"Open it," she commanded, her eyes glowing under the shade of the ridiculous rain hat.

I began to open it. "Why can't we do this in the . . ."

There was a loud *pop!*

The top of the ketchup bottle exploded off. I stood

there wet and stunned. I looked down at Sunny. Her
rain gear was covered in ketchup. I looked down at
myself. Ketchup was splashed across my T-shirt and
jeans in giant blobs, and it streamed down my face
and neck in ketchupy gobs.

"Oh my gosh," I breathed. "Sunny, are you okay?" I wiped at the ketchup on her coat, but it didn't smear. In fact, it just stayed there. "Holy mother of peanuts!" I wiped at the ketchup on my arm. It also stayed. "Why isn't this coming off?" I looked down at my little sister.

"It's not going to come off," she said excitedly. "It's a special red dye I invented."

"What?"

"Well, it will come off, but just not for a few days. It has to wear off."

"WHAT? You mean you did this on purpose?"

She shook her head, smiling, happy that I had finally gotten it. "Yes, Masha. You see, you are the person not following the rules of society. You will walk around the science fair covered in weird red blotches and I will observe how people react to you. *You're my science experiment!*"

Sunny unsnapped the rain jacket and stuffed it into her box. Her jeans and T-shirt were spotless. "Okay," she said. "Let's go."

"Let's go?" I said. I was standing in some random

school's parking lot a million miles from home covered from head to toe in "weird red blotches." I could
feel the anger gurgling up inside me. I guess Sunny
could feel it too, because she took a slow step away
from me.

I lunged . . . but that tiny little twig body of hers
was too quick, and she took off toward the front doors
of the building.

"SUNNY SWEET," I screamed, "YOU ARE SO
DEAD MEAT!"

Acknowledgments

I would like to thank . . .

My husband, Kevin Mann, for his never-ending support of my wish to write, even through some pretty grim times.

My children, Jackson Mann and Grace Mann, for putting up with a mother with a dream.

My agent, Kerry Sparks, for possessing the killer combination of patience and tenacity.

My editor, Caroline Abbey, who read everything I ever sent her, waiting for this one.